UNDERWORLDS

Tales of Paranormal Lust

mischief

This novel is entirely a work of fiction.
The names, characters and incidents portrayed in it are
the work of the author's imagination. Any resemblance to
actual persons, living or dead, events or localities is
entirely coincidental.

Mischief
An imprint of HarperCollins*Publishers*
77–85 Fulham Palace Road,
Hammersmith, London W6 8JB

www.mischiefbooks.com

A Paperback Original 2013

First published in Great Britain in ebook format by
HarperCollins*Publishers* 2012

A catalogue record for this book is
available from the British Library

ISBN-13: 9780007553181

Find out more about HarperCollins and the environment at
www.harpercollins.co.uk/green

Contents

CONTENTS

Heavenly Shades
Charlotte Stein

I can hear the prickle of a needle on vinyl from all the way up here, but this time I don't flinch. My heart doesn't try to scramble out of my chest. Instead, I just let myself float here, in the tepid water now filling my bathtub. I drift, like an island of perfectly slick, pale flesh.

While downstairs the music cycles up. First the violins, looping along one after the other. Then that crushed-velvet voice, pouring out of the record player and all the way up to me. *Heavenly shades of night are falling*, the singer croons, as I let my hand flow back and forth in the water. *It's twilight time*, the song continues, and then I know for certain.

He is here.

It's like his calling card, I suppose. The cue for him to enter stage right. That shushing beat starts, and after it come his footsteps on the stairs. Heavy and slumberous, somehow, even though he is neither.

He's as quick as a snake and barely past six foot, body like a whip. Face like one, too. If I hadn't seen underneath his clothes I'd think he was a pointed finger, muscle-less and mean. But I know different, now. I didn't want to, but I do anyway.

And I suppose that's the way of things, with him.

I don't want to get out of the bathtub and put on the nightgown he gave me for such special occasions. I don't want to wait for him in my bedroom, as pretty and clean as a picture.

But I do it anyway. In fact, I do more than that. I dry my hair, and brush it out into one long spill down my back. And then finally I look in the mirror, as I always do, and try to think what makes my face the one. What made him look at me and think: It's her I'll do this to. Not sunny Kelli Fisher, from number thirty-six. Not Mrs Levine, who's still lovely and lissom and not half as plain as me. My face is like a blank slate, empty of anything that could move a man to madness. My eyes are like stones, my mouth is a barely there imprint.

And yet he comes to me all the same. He's there when I pad across the hall and enter my entirely alien bedroom. It used to be a place of comfort in here; everything in it used to be familiar to me. But now it looks like the funhouse version of that space, shadows striping things at odd angles. Pictures hung where they shouldn't be. The full moon barely penetrating into the room, even though I know that shouldn't be the case. I know its light should be more than this weak little blurred thing that creeps over my carpet and scarcely touches my toes.

It's like he drives it away somehow.

It's like he drives my will away, too.

'Come and dance with me, my little bird, my little one in particular,' he says, and I think of those words over and over, as I force my feet over the carpet to him. *My one in particular*, he always says, because I'm special, I'm so special.

So why is it that I sob against his shoulder the minute he takes me in his arms?

Because I do. I make a sound like something dying and let myself sag into him, that strange wired strength in him holding me up, even as I try to sink down to the floor. I suspect he could hold me up if I was as heavy as twenty bags of concrete. I suspect he could lead me around like this, boneless and doll-like, if I fought with all of my might.

I fought the first time, after all. All the way back then, when I had only suspected. He'd come over to borrow a cup of sugar, and I'd thought to myself, half-giddily: If he really is some kind of creature of the night, he won't be able to come into the house – so don't invite him in.

And I hadn't. Instead, I'd just tentatively passed the cup over the high holy threshold, waiting for him to reach forward and take it. And then, when he had, I'd done the worst possible thing I could have. The thing that caused all of this, the thing that made it be so.

I'd pulled the cup back at the last second, and watched him press his fingers to the invisible barrier blocking his way, as though it were a pane of glass.

It was too late for me then; I understand that now. He knew that I knew, from that moment on, and from that moment on my only job was to evade him – and I did. I raced the daylight home every day after it happened, but there's always more twilight. There's always more night waiting to descend on me at just the wrong moment, and it had descended even faster after he put that hole in my gas line.

Because he's clever, you see. He's not like the ones you see in movies, who creak out of their coffins and hypnotise you in nightclubs. He has to use his wiles, rather than some set of hoary old mystical clichés. He has to rely on a serial killer's tricks to snare his prey.

And he snared me well. I walked all the way home from the middle of nowhere, knowing what he'd done. Knowing, but unable to do anything about it. The darkness had fallen so fast, and I simply wasn't capable of running the five miles home.

Even if I had, I wouldn't have made it in time. I *didn't* make it in time.

And so here we are, dancing to the music I hear no matter where I am or what I'm doing. In the supermarket, trembling and near bloodless from the night before. Always tired now, always so weak, my mind drifting to the sound of that slowly dripping song, and his face. His eyes, like burned syrup.

'Please,' I say. 'Please.'

But I'm praying to the wrong God. This one has hair like a raven's wing and hands as cold as stones at the bottom of an icy river, and when I beg him to give me my life back he just murmurs *shhhh, shhhh*, in a way that should be soothing.

And it almost is. Everything he does is almost soothing, almost tender – like a lover trying to coax me into the most sensuous bout of lovemaking. One hand pressed to my lower back, rubbing and rubbing there. The other in my hair, stroking so softly it makes me sob again.

It's so *close* to something sweet, I think. So close I could almost believe in it, if it were not for the true purpose behind the thrust of his fingers through the newly cleaned strands.

He doesn't like it to get in his way, when he gets a mouthful of me.

'Oh, my little one,' he says against the side of my face. But even without looking I know the teeth are there. I can almost feel the steely press of them as he comes close to kissing me, and as his breath ghosts, cool and strange, all over my skin.

'Don't,' I say again, but the word is small and fluttering

and he is powerful, so powerful. I can feel the twist of those muscles beneath the hand I'm pushing against his shoulder – though it's more than that. He's like a steel cage, in a way no man should ever be. He locks me in tight, and, though he coos and murmurs and tries to calm me down, in the end he always has to force it.

He holds me fast, that hand in my hair now like a vice. And, though I know what's coming, I still squeeze my eyes tight shut for it. I brace myself, and then there's just his icy mouth against my throat. That eagerness in him, suddenly – despite the fact that he's never eager for anything.

He's always slow, so slow and deliberate. After he'd caught me that first time, he stalked me like some crouching, clever beast that doesn't actually exist. A raptor, I always think, but there's nothing lizard-like about him – apart from the cold. And when you look at him, that cold isn't there at all.

He looks heated, primal somehow. His hips practically rolled, as he backed me into a corner. And the second I tried to evade him by doing something stupid – like jumping into the swimming pool he never uses; of course he never uses it – he just walked right into the water as though it wasn't even a step down.

Where are you going, Francesca, he'd said, like I was so silly to want to get away.

And I suppose he had a point. There's no getting away,

from him. I just have to hang there helpless in his arms, as his lips part and that razor sharpness grazes my skin. Every inch of me waiting for the worst feeling – the one the movies never suggest.

It's like a *crunch*. His teeth slide into me and then there's the strangest sensation afterwards ... like he's breaking my bones, somehow, even though I know he isn't. There's never more than two puncture marks on my skin afterwards, and no side-effects apart from the lethargy.

But that first shot of pain, so intense it's almost like pleasure ...

It's unbearable. It's unstoppable. It's like a side-effect in its own way, because even when I'm alone I can remember and feel it almost exactly.

But the pain right now is remarkable, even by those standards. It narrows my body down to that one bright focus point, until I have to do something unbearable like gasp, harsh and guttural, at the ceiling, tears spilling in an entirely different way down my cheeks.

This time they come like a reflex, with barely any sadness behind them at all. And if I say his name at the same time, well, isn't that like a reflex, too? Isn't it like the begging I always do before he sinks his teeth in?

'Merrith,' I say, because he'd told me it once, after the blood had made him lazy and satisfied. Vulnerable, I always think, but that's not true at all. He just seems it when he cradles my limp body against his, and tells me things I'm sure he never tells anyone else. Everyone else thinks he's Jimmy Brecker, but he isn't really. He's Merrith, just Merrith, as though he came from a time beyond surnames and Christian names.

Maybe he really did, I think, as my life flows out of me and into him. And though it's painful, this is the part where a different sort of sensation starts to take over. A pulling sensation, like he's got a hand on some thread inside me and he's just easing it on through.

It's as debilitating, in its own way, as the bone-crushing first bite. It turns my legs to jelly; it makes me faint and fearful of myself. Sometimes I almost drift off like this, and there's the ever-present terror that I'm never actually going to wake up again.

But there's something else there, too. Sometimes I come around and I'm clinging to him in the same way he clings to me – like a lover, not a victim. One arm looped around his shoulders; a hand stroking down over the perfect curve of his spine. Every sense I've got so aware of my own body, as it turns to water in his arms.

By the time he's done, I'm no longer standing. He's holding me like this, with my pointed feet nearly all the way off the floor. And when he takes his first big breath – like a little kid would do, after drinking too much lemonade – I feel his body shuddering against the whole length of mine.

'So sweet,' he says, once he's capable of speech. 'So sweet when you let me have you like this.'

And though I try to tell myself not to, I think of the dual meaning of *have*. Of course I do – it's like a compulsion, after all this time, of his hands and his mouth and the music, rich and strange. I sag against his shoulder and think of those liquid eyes of his, always searching through me like a hand sifting through pretty things.

'My one,' he says, and then he just licks long and languid over the still bleeding bits of me – everything about the move so tender that my mind immediately turns to animals, and the way they heal each other.

Is that what he is, really? An animal underneath, reacting to things in a blind, instinctive way? And, if so, is it really so bad if I do the same?

Because it's perfectly true that I don't know what I'm doing, when I push my fingers into his thick dark hair. It's like I've lapsed into that heavy state of unconsciousness, even though I'm still awake. I understand that I'm still awake, as I hold that suddenly warm and wet mouth to my throat.

Of course I expect him to resume that hypnotic pulling – or at the very least to keep licking me in that way I don't like at all, I swear I don't. But instead he makes this sound that I don't recognise – as though I've startled him – and arches away from me. Gets my face in one long-fingered hand, so that he can look down into my eyes.

9

'You want me to?' he asks, and for a second I'm sure he means the other thing. The one that I never think of, when he gets his hand on that thread and pulls. But then he carries on in that startled and completely new tone, those eyes of his suddenly naked. 'You want me to taste you?'

And I think, Yes, yes, but not in the way you're imagining.

Of course I know it's too late then for me. Like when I made the choice to try to catch him out, and his fingers pushed against the invisible glass. I've pushed my fingers against an invisible barrier and just kept on going right through to the other side, where my hands are full of his hair and my body is completely aware of all the things he never does.

In truth, I'm not even sure if he knows what those things are any more – instead, there's just a hole in him, where desire and lust and pleasure used to be. It's like knowing someone who never needs to breathe. At some point, you expect them to want to. You expect them to suddenly jolt with the memory of something that once kept them living.

But he doesn't. He doesn't even remember when I reverse what he's been doing to me. He just hangs there in my arms, blankly staring, and lets me put my mouth on his. Lets me taste my own blood in his mouth, and come away just as he always does: streaked with red, stunned by the sensation of feeding.

10

But, unlike him, I don't let myself lapse into that oddly vulnerable state. I don't tell him my real name – what would be the point? He already knows it. And I don't let him curl against me, to chase away the confusion and hurt all over his face.

I just do it again, in all the different ways I can think of to kiss. Open-mouthed and close-mouthed and soft and wet. Then maybe all of those things together, until he does something that shocks me more than his vampirism ever did.

He kisses me back. He kisses me back, as though he does know how to breathe after all. It's just like riding a bike, I think, deliriously, but there's another simile just hovering on the edges of my mind. One I don't want to think about, at first, but then – isn't that what I've been doing along?

I've refused to think about those hands on my back, roaming and running over me in the way they do again now. I've refused to think about the song, like the sort of thing you'd put on if you wanted to seduce a girl. I've refused to think of the word *one*, and what it usually means in romance novels.

But I think of all of these things now, because when I put my mouth on him all of them are reframed entirely. It's not just a hint. It's right there in my face – that his hands make me so swollen and slippery, between my legs. That the feel of his body against mine stiffens my nipples, whether I want it to or not.

11

And it's not just because he's a man, underneath it all. It's because his name is Merrith, I think. It's because he stares and stares at me as though I've suddenly become some entirely different creature, and the longer he does the stronger that feeling gets between my legs. Usually it's just this syrupy sort of thing, born of the pulling sensation and the laxness and some internal confusion.

But now I can actually make it out distinctly, and put a name to it without shame. I'm aroused. I'm aroused because of the things he does to me, and because of that sense of an absent need in him. He doesn't even know what sex is any more – but that's all right.

I do.

'It's like this,' I tell him, and then I take his hand just as the music cycles back up again. I slip my fingers around his waist, and lead him into a different sort of dance.

One that ends up on the bed.

Of course, he doesn't do any of the things you're supposed to, once we're there. He doesn't tear my clothes off, or tear his clothes off, or rut against me frantically – though it doesn't matter really. There's at least one of us doing all of those things, as greedily as I've ever felt myself be.

In fact, I'm not even sure if I *have* ever been this greedy. My fingers feel oddly numb and fumbly, unable to do something as simple as make my body naked. And when I try to do the same thing to him, the effect is tripled.

12

Quadrupled. I'm practically paralysed by the sight of so much of him, so pale he's almost translucent. Every muscle and line in exactly the right place, even though I'd kind of expected to uncover something strange.

Like maybe he'd turn out to be a satyr or worse, underneath his clothes. There'd be fur in all the places I haven't yet seen, and hooves where his feet should be – but of course there's none of that. He's perfectly formed, perfectly man-shaped, and more than this … he's remembering fast, for someone who seems so dazed.

Between his legs he's thick and stiff. And though I suppose it should be this that frightens me, it isn't. It's the other thing, it's the *crunch*, it's the bitter bleakness of having that hole in my gas line and seeing the night come down, down, down. Whereas this, by comparison …

This is something I'm asking for. It's the first thing I've asked for. And it seems the moment I do, he's willing to give it. He even runs one cool hand over the length of my spread body, in an echo of the thing I do to him the moment I have the chance. I just reach up and feel every inch of his skin, feel his cock all perfectly right and normal, and in response he touches me there, too.

Between my legs, I mean.

And when he does, it's so soft, so soft it's almost too much. It's the reverse again of everything that's come before – or at least I think it is, until I go back over it all. I think about his mouth again, and his teeth, and the way he held me, as he slides one finger through my slippery slit in the very same manner.

Steadily, slowly, with deliberation, I think. I'm an animal he needs to calm and make still before he can stroke it. Before he can map it out with curious fingers – because, God, that's what it feels like.

I'm being mapped out. He needs to rediscover everything, like the exact shape of my stiff clit. He just follows all the grooves and folds surrounding it, everything getting steadily slicker until I know I should be embarrassed.

But I'm not. I'm not even embarrassed when he finds my greedy cunt and eases just one finger in, all slow and slippery, working back and forth before I've had the chance to really consider – and when I do, they aren't normal thoughts. Yeah, I think, when he twists those digits inside me and finds some good good place. Fuck my tight little pussy.

Whereas his responses are the innocent ones, for once. The expression on his face is near-startled, almost curious – as though he hadn't realised a woman could be all slick there like this. And he absolutely didn't know that I could squirm for him and moan for him and urge him to do it harder.

'Is this what you are asking me for?' he says, but it isn't in the voice I've come to know. There's an accent there now, somewhere behind the false façade of his American one. A thick one, a guttural one, that runs right out of his mouth and all over my body, a second before his hand follows it.

He's caressing me now, I think, but of course doing so makes answering him hard. All I want to focus on is how his hands feel – the one that's stroking my breasts as though he's actually and gradually coming to know what this all means, and the one that remains between my legs, rubbing and rubbing in that maddening way.

Until I say: 'Yes.'

And then after he just leans down, as slow as syrup. That curious, questioning look so clear on his face, a moment before he does something that makes me cover my eyes with my hands. I can't watch, I just can't – though of course I realise a moment later what those words mean.

They're what the heroine of a horror movie would say, just before she sees a loved one being eaten by the creature from beyond. It's what I should have said, when he first stalked towards me, teeth bared.

But I didn't. Instead, I do it now, as he licks one long stripe through my spread sex. I cover my eyes and imagine running up the stairs rather than going out the front door, while he tastes me in the same way he recently tasted my blood. Greedily, so greedily, and with just enough finesse to make me twist on the bed.

It won't take long, I think. I'm even further out onto that edge than I imagined I was, though I swear I didn't imagine much of it at all. I never pictured him rubbing that red, red tongue back and forth over my swollen clit. I didn't think he'd ever want me to cry out in something other than fear or pain – but I do.

'Merrith,' I say, and I don't do it quietly. It rings out over the ever-repeating song, so loud and so obvious that I'm sure he's going to stop now. He's going to take it away from me again, and go back to the way things were. He's tried this and found it wanting, even if his grasping hands and his hungry, generous mouth suggest otherwise.

He's almost eating at me, now. I can feel the glancing edge of his teeth whenever he insinuates his mouth through my folds. I can feel his hot breath rushing over me, when he licks and licks over the entrance to my cunt – as though he can't wait for more now. He has to stuff it all into his mouth, quick, before it comes to the only kind of ending it can.

I'm going to die of pleasure, I know it. I'm too weak to resist, too weak to do anything but lie here and feel this bloom of sensation in my sex, working its way up through my body until it has me around the throat. And when it finally does come, and I arch my back for it and cry his name again, I'm almost stunned to find that at the end I'm still conscious.

My eyes are closed and I'm barely breathing, but I'm here, I'm here. I'm alive and I remain so, in those arms that go around me. He doesn't try to bite me again, or force me into some strange perverted memory he has of what sex is supposed to be.

He just takes me like that, on my back, slow and almost languorous. Each thrust like rolling thunder, while the needle scratches and scratches on the record and the crooner tells the tale for me. *Heavenly shades of night are falling*, he sings, just as I dig my nails into Merrith's back. They make a little popping sound as they pierce his flesh, so faint you could almost miss it.

Though of course my vampire doesn't. He hisses for me instead and bares his teeth, but now they're blunt and harmless – not so scary any more. And when I bare my own teeth back at him he retreats, just a little, even as my body keeps him right where he is.

I've drawn blood now. I've held him tight inside my slick heat, and though he makes a show of resisting I can hear that sigh in the back of his throat. I know what the expression on his face means – I've seen it a hundred times before.

'Please,' he says to me, like the last little dot on the final i of the contract.

And then I roll my hips, just so. I work myself on his cock, over and over, until the pleasure swells through me as fiercely as it did a moment ago – only better this time. Sweeter. I feel him cling to me as it takes me down, because he's drowning, too.

'I'd forgotten,' he tells me, in his new voice – as the pleasure makes him arch his back and jerk his hips too hard against my still swollen sex. 'I'd forgotten.'

But he doesn't have to tell me about that. I know what forgetting is.

I used to be human, after all.

But now I don't even remember what that is.

Slave of the Lamp
Janine Ashbless

*Rub it! Rub it harder! Oh – oh, yes! Don't stop! Yes,
I'm coming!*

In an indigo-hued cloud I gush forth from the neck of
the Lamp, swelling immensely. Flesh thickens into solidity
as it contacts the air. New skin, the colour of a twilight
sky, webs across sheets of muscle. I open my just-formed
mouth to take great breaths, smelling wild sage and dust,
incense and cardamom and the hated stink of humanity.
Then I stretch my limbs and groan with the indescribable
pleasure of incarnation.

There's plenty of room to stretch. I am outdoors this
time. As I blink my eyes into focus I see I'm standing
in a broad valley walled by yellow hills. Around me
kneel the Children of Earth, their faces hidden in their
sleeves. They are so small that I might crush one into
the dirt with the ball of my bare foot, and I laugh in

19

contempt. My shout booms from the cliff faces.

'Djinni!' Only one figure does not kneel or avert her gaze. She stands in her royal robes under a canopy, surrounded by a sea of bowed heads, and she looks at me without flinching. Her hair is like the mane of a lion, though the pelt across her shoulder is that of a leopard. A broad collar of gold lies upon her breasts, and in her hands sits the Lamp.

Bilqis: Queen of the Land of Sheba. Under the necklace, the jut of her breasts is most enticing to the eye.

'Djinni,' she says, in that throaty voice, 'you should appear in more seemly guise.'

I glance down at myself, pleased by what I see. Every inch of my flesh thrills to the sensation of release from confinement, my male member no less than the rest. It stands as solid as the central pillar of a temple, and as blue as a storm cloud. I grasp it in my fist, caressing it lovingly, rediscovering that particular pleasure.

'Does it not please you, mistress?' I ask, grinning at her. My cock is hot and full, and so hard that if I lay upon a mountaintop I could prop up the dome of the sky with it. And it has not escaped my notice that the mortal queen stands almost exactly as tall as it does. I might wear her as an ornament. That mental picture is gratifying.

She jerks her head, and I am pleased to have discomfited her. I give myself a stroke and my cock springs back and slaps against the hard wall of my stomach.

'Cover yourself!' she mouths. Then, louder: 'I command it.'

I shrug, trying not to show my prickling irritation. I cannot disobey, of course. She summoned me from the Lamp, and I am its slave. With the mere lift of an eyebrow I attire myself in loose turquoise-blue trousers, then I tuck my swollen glans behind the waistband. I put my fists on my hips, largely to stop me reaching down and sweeping into ruin the whole verminous swarm at my feet. 'Your every whim is as divine law to me, mistress,' I say silkily.

She relaxes a little. She is beautiful – no longer with the fawn-like charm of youth, to be sure, but lushly curved – yet she stands upon her modesty among men, as I remember. I comprehend how my naked masculinity must disturb the peace of her woman's mind, like a wild bull rampaging through a tidy garden.

'I have a task for you, djinni,' she says.

A baby wails.

My interest sharpens as I recall that she was pregnant the last time I saw her, though now her womb is empty. Looking among the entourage crouching in the dirt, I spot the small form cradled in the crook of a nursemaid's arm. It appears to be trying to escape from its captivity. The girl pulls it to her anxiously.

'Is that the child?' I ask, my voice a rumble like distant thunder. 'Is that the get of Solomon the Wise?' It is hard to conceal my loathing of that name and Bilqis casts a sharp, maternal glance over her shoulder, bristling.

'He is my son,' she says. 'And it is my command that you never bring him to harm.'

'A son?' I laugh, wanting to hurt. 'After sixty generations of queens in Sheba?'

'My son,' she repeats, warningly. 'And he will be great among the kings of the world. And you will kneel before him. Now.'

I clench my teeth. Then I sink to my knees and press my forehead to the earth. I have no choice.

'Djinni,' she says, mollified, 'I have a task for you.'

'Mistress.'

'Vizier, show him the plans.'

I raise myself to hands and knees in order to look down at a bent old man with a grey beard, who comes forward unfurling a scroll. He looks like he is about to soil his silk robe in fear. He can't even look me in the face. On the parchment is a picture of what seems to be a wall.

'Do you see?' says Bilqis. 'I want you to build me a dam right across the Wadi Dhana here. To those measurements. With sluice gates at either end, as depicted – so that, when the river runs full again, water may be trapped here and used to irrigate the land around. Do you understand, djinni? It must be built of stone and fit to stand for a thousand years. That is my command.'

I dig my talons into the sand. But part of me recognises that I would rather be out here, even slaving as a menial builder for her, than be confined again inside the Lamp. It is a welcome respite.

'To hear, mistress, is to obey.'

* * *

I was a parting gift. Imagine that, if you can! King Solomon gave me to her as a slave, the day she gathered up her entourage and set out from Jerusalem on the long journey home. She carried another farewell present inside her belly that day, though I do not think he knew about that. The unformed seedling in her belly was a blazing fire to my eye, but I was certainly not about to volunteer any such information to him.

The arrogance of the man takes my breath away still. He'd had lamps of brass and gold made to hang in his palace – each one the shape of a tear, as if the sun itself had wept. Into each lamp he'd bound one of my brothers or sisters, so that their undying flames might illuminate his stinking slovenly rooms. Can you comprehend such an obscenity – the Firstborn, the Children of Fire, the Lords of the Sky and the Earth, imprisoned and made to light up the corners of some miserable little sandstone palace in a backwater shit-hole? I, who have stood upon the ziggurats of Uruk and Harappa and Babylon, and had emperors cast their crowns at my feet! I, who have walked the Walls of the Earth, and looked over into the star-strewn void!

Solomon the Wise, eh? Solomon the *Sorcerer*. His people profess to abhor the magical arts, but he is the most cunning, ruthless and puissant of wizards. He has dug secrets out of the underworld and tricked the divine names from the lips of angels.

Bilqis knows all that, of course. She sought him out because his wisdom and learning were renowned, even among the maggot-headed Children of Earth. She tested him with her riddles – yes, we watched that from our prisons; the two of them sitting up long into the night, sparring verbally – and when he passed her test she lay with him to get a child worthy to be her own heir. Oh yes: a wise sorcerer-king for the great realm of Sheba; that was what she desired. The moment she knew she was carrying, she was out of that place. Before he could imprison her too, I do not doubt, and keep the child for his own.

I do not want to think about him. Remembrance fills me with such ire that the binding spells he wrought upon me – those words he etched onto my skin – burn and gnaw at my flesh, searing me to the bone. If I could, I would tear off my hide and incinerate it in the inner fires of the Earth, and then I would be free of him.

But what is written is written.

* * *

24

She summons me forth once more. This time I am indoors, and cannot grow to my full height. I rein myself in before I smash through the carved cedar beams of the roof.

There is a squealing and a shrieking, a flurry of panic at my arrival. I look down and see the room is full of women. It makes me grin to see them shrink away and cover their faces – though several are peeking through the slits of their fingers, and that makes me grin too. I have arrived clothed, because Bilqis commands me thus, but my silken trousers do not fully disguise the extent of my exuberance. They are all young and lovely; their breasts bare and firm, their shapely thighs and rounded bottoms a field of delight that my rampant share urges me to plough. In Solomon's palace, I would assume that this is the apartment of his concubines. Here in Sheba, they must be the queen's handmaidens. It is clear they have not been expecting the arrival of any male, and their consternation is enchanting. I wish to rush in among them like a cockerel among a flock of hens.

'Djinni!'

I force my attention back to Bilqis, who kneels upon cushions in the middle of this fluttering crowd, with a slender maiden cradled in her arms. 'Mistress?'

She's dressed less formally today. I can see her ebony nipples through the damp and clinging gauze of her robe. I understand that the land of Sheba is considered punishingly hot by humans. 'Djinni,' says she, 'my slave here has been bitten by a viper. Can you heal her?'

The girl in her arms is twisting with pain, her dark skin grey now and glistening with sweat. I can see her injured foot, swollen to twice its natural size, propped upon a cushion.

'Pray to the God of Solomon, mistress,' I suggest sourly. 'Does He not promise to be merciful?'

'I have. And to Shams and Ilmaqah and Athtar, who rule this land. The gods do not answer me. So if it lies within your power, djinni, I command you to heal this maid.'

I briefly consider some way to twist her words, but my heart is not in it. I am too distracted by the perfumed, quivering throng of women. And the girl is pretty, for a human, or will be so when well. I twitch a single finger – mostly to show how easy this is for me – and the poison hisses out of her, issuing as a faint green cloud from her open lips. Her leg reverts instantly to healthy flesh.

Everyone in the room utters a *wahwahwah* of wonder. Except Bilqis, who smiles and nods, and the girl, who sobs and buries her face in her queen's breasts.

'There, there,' says the monarch of all Sheba, both left and right of the Red Sea. 'You are fine. No need to cry, my sweet one.'

And my eyes widen as the maid pulls down the fine gauze of the queen's robe and sucks a big nipple into her mouth.

Bilqis closes her own eyes for a moment in pleasure, then opens them, meeting my gaze with a long, considering look. 'You did well, djinni,' she says. 'It pleases me to reward you.' With a couple of clicks of her fingers she jerks two of the women at the side of the chamber from their knees. 'You two: see to his pleasure.'

I'm taken aback, but far from dismayed. The young women are curvaceous of body and beautiful of face, and they advance towards me with rapidly rising and falling breasts, bright-eyed but gratifyingly nervous.

'It would help, djinni,' says the queen in a dry voice, 'if you were to assume the size of a mortal man.'

I comply, shrinking my towering form down from the ceiling, until I am only the size of a *very large* man. The two handmaidens kneel before me on the cushioned floor, and reach for my hidden weapon, wetting their lips as they tug at my clothes. They are eager to obey their queen, I note, approving.

'Do not hurt them, djinni,' Bilqis adds as an afterthought.

I bare my sharp teeth in a grin at her. But I clasp my wrists at the small of my back, safely out of the way.

Then the handmaids lay hold of their prize; one cupping my big balls, the other stroking my thick shaft. Both of them vie for the right to suck my glans, and most stimulating it is to watch them fight for the honour; their lips wrestling over the crown of my manhood, their tongues lashing and sliding over the veined pillar of my magnificence. Teasing fingers stroke my balls and the skin behind. I let out a groan of appreciation. These two are not ignorant of the bodies of men, clearly.

And it is so long since I have known carnal pleasure. Years now, trapped in that Lamp. My sap rises swiftly. I look up from the two bobbing heads at my crotch, just to distance myself and prolong the delight, but the broader view does not provide distraction. Every woman in that room is watching me, looking at my body and my cock and their two sisters sucking and slurping at it. Their eyes are wide, drinking in the sight. Their full, moist lips are parted. Their soft breasts heave with each breath they take. Some look entranced; some wary; some hungry. Even the queen herself wears a faint smile, though the maid she is suckling at her breasts is kissing with such vigour that Bilqis' expression appears somewhat unfocused.

My bow is at full stretch, straining for release. I can feel my balls tighten, their hot wet burden ready to be spilled. My thighs are so taut they tremble. I look down once more and see my two handmaidens are taking it in turn to run their tongues up the length of my cock, each swallowing the head, sucking it lovingly, and then letting it go just in time for the other girl to engulf it.

'Yes, oh yes,' I growl, fire swimming in my veins. 'That is right, you Whores of the Earth! This is your place, all of you!'

'Stop,' says Bilqis sharply.

In an instant the two girls draw away, leaving my cock standing bereft and waving wetly. My vision swims. I can feel the flame burning in my blood turn to pain. I can feel my balls clenching. I turn to the queen with a snarl.

'I give, and I take away,' Bilqis says, brushing the girl from her as she stands. The queen has a wrathful glitter in her eye. 'Get back into your Lamp, djinni.'

I have no choice but to obey.

* * *

Inside my prison it is not cramped. Or at least, it's not a constriction of the body, there being no body in this place. But it is dark, and it is lonely. I may light it with suns and build within it worlds of my imagining, but the mind grows weary in time. I walk the star-strewn halls of artifice and replay the wild events of memory, but I speak to no one but myself.

I understand that the Children of Earth dream, and in their dreaming minds meet with those who are not themselves – gods and tricksters, lost friends and the forgotten dead. It is not like that for the Djinn. We do not dream.

It is possible for me to look out from my cell, and see all that the wavering flame at the tip illuminates. But Bilqis has me kept in an empty room, and I rarely bother.

I create in my prison a woman of gold who moves and walks and does as I command her, and I fashion her in the form of my captor. Upon that golden body I heap every indignity I can conceive of – but without the sensations of the flesh, and without her having will or thought or speech of her own, there is no satisfaction in it and no release for me. I burn, and I will burn for ever. My Lamp will never go out.

* * *

The next time Bilqis calls me from my prison, the hand of night lies upon the Earth. I stand in a chamber I have never seen before, which contains a great bed. There are only three women in the room this time. Two are entirely naked, and they may not have noticed my entrance at all, because the first is lying back upon the coverlet and the other has her face buried in the girl's sex and is lapping away – to some effect, judging from the hitch and twitch of those hips and the way the reclining maid is panting as she plays with her own breasts.

'Djinni,' says the third, the queen herself, 'I have something to show you. Stand and watch. Do not move until I tell you.'

It is not an entirely disagreeable command, for once. Bilqis is clad only in a collar of bright feathers and a belt of lapis lazuli beads. They glow against the dark shimmer of her skin, drawing attention to its velvet softness, to the curve of her waist and the swell of her heavy breasts. But there is no vulnerability in her near-nakedness; she holds herself regally, as if in coronation robes.

She rises and places the Lamp safely aside upon a shelf, and then from under a cushion on the bed – she reaches around the two labouring handmaids, stroking both idly with her fingertips – she fetches an apparatus that I do not, at first, comprehend. It consists of two phalluses, shaped from stitched and stiffened leather, joined at a peculiar angle. There are many soft straps too, and Bilqis fastens these about her hips and thighs, sliding the more curved of the two false members deep inside her. When she tightens the harness and straightens, the second cock stands out from her pubic mound – for all the world like a true erection, if a woman could sport such a thing. It looks obscene. She strokes it lovingly, dipping her fingers into a bowl of perfumed oil to lavish her slippery caress upon the thick shaft. She pumps it with her fist as if it might ejaculate.

I do not know whether to be amused or affronted. She is a mockery of all that is a man – and yet my own cock twitches; I find this sight strangely arousing. More so when, ignoring me, she kneels up upon the bed and touches the supine handmaid upon the peak of her breast.

The girl opens her eyes, gazing up at her queen with a look of naked adoration. First she stretches up to kiss the slippery shaft, then she rolls over onto her front, drawing her knees beneath her to raise her ass. Presented like that, it appears as an exquisite heart-shape. The girl who has been doing the licking slides her hands into those of the kneeling girl and grips her tight, as a comrade offering comfort.

Oh, how I ache.

The queen ... the queen is kneeling up behind that luscious rear, her hands on those hips. The phallus is angled right at the maiden's well-licked sex. That cleft must be puffy and wet and open by now; it certainly seems to offer no resistance as the blunt helmet noses into it and the shaft follows, disappearing inch by inch into the hot depths. The queen works her hips with consummate care, biting her lip as she surges and then slacks. Her eyes are half-hooded, her sapphire-painted lids fluttering with each push of her thighs, each heave of her glorious breasts. The handmaiden below whimpers and gasps, twisting her own hips as she makes room for the obdurate prod invading her innermost parts. I struggle to understand what is happening – surely the queen can feel nothing through that false manhood?

Then I realise that each thrust must press upon the sensitive nub of her sex, and grind the second phallus into her own passage. It seems to be sufficient to bring her satisfaction. There is a glow rising in the queen's cheeks as she labours, and a trembling jerkiness to her move-ments, just as the girl's groans are becoming deeper and wilder. Bilqis' breasts shudder, and the wobbling dance of those delectable orbs with their staring nipples is almost enough to distract me from the unnatural fucking going on beneath. Almost, but not quite. The undulation of all that feminine flesh quivering and slapping together is making the hot blood throb in my cock.

I would show them how it is done, if I were free.

Then Bilqis begins to gasp, her hands biting into the girl's flesh, her thrusts suddenly commendably savage. The girl wails – though not, I think, in protest; she is pressing back upon her queen's weapon – and in a flurry of shudders and two mingled cries of release it is over.

A smile upon her flushed face, Bilqis detaches the thigh-straps of the harness and steps down from the bed, leaving the phallic apparatus still buried in the pretty slave-girl. 'Was that instructive, djinni?'

'Most enlightening, mistress.' How I burn to use the harlot, just as she used the maid.

With a slap upon that bottom, she commands, 'Leave now,' and I watch as the two girls rise obediently and slip out of the room. Then she comes over to me. Her eyes are full of unassuaged lasciviousness. Oftentimes, my brother djinn have taken mortal women as concubines. Their own men, it is said, are unable to satisfy their great appetites, which is why they cannot remain faithful to their lawful husbands. Bilqis, I think, is one of those women.

She puts her hand upon the bar of my engorged member. With a grin I make myself naked once more, so that there is nothing between her skin and mine. She glances down, admiring, as she strokes my shaft, and my chest swells with triumph as my cock-slit weeps with joy.

'Djinni,' says she, 'I want a cock.'

I am taken aback. I laugh to cover my dismay. 'Would you be a man, then?' I mock her. 'Is it not enough to be queen, that you must be king?'

She steps back, eyeing my frustration with undisguised amusement. 'Why would I want to be a man?' she asks, running her hands over her own body, caressing the rich curves of hip and waist, hefting and cupping and squeezing her breasts until my eyes feel like they will burst from my head. 'A man spends his pleasure once, and then is done. I may take mine over and over, with every woman in my harem. But ...' She licks her lips. 'I want to be able to feel it when I enter my favourite's tight hole. I want to be a woman, yet with a cock of flesh. I want one like yours.'

I don't know what to say. It appals me, and it excites me in ways I cannot describe.

'I command it, djinni,' she says, looking in my eyes.

So I give her a cock. And, as an afterthought, a pouch of balls, because I think it looks better that way, and they will suit her. She steps back with a gasp, touching herself, her fingers like fluttering butterflies.

Her member is already half-hard; it becomes harder as she grasps and strokes it, harder in great surges. She casts me a look of disbelief, which I do not understand because this is what she asked for. Then she checks between her legs to make sure I have not robbed her of her woman's parts.

'You have both, mistress,' I say through gritted teeth. 'As you desired. Though you will not sow any seed with that thing.'

'Then it is for pleasure only,' she says, and there is a fire in her eyes when she looks upon me that seems to belong to the Flameborn, not the Children of Dust. 'Lie upon the bed, djinni.'

'Me?' I stutter. Outrage flares through my soul.

'You, djinni.' She smirks. 'I command it.'

'No!' I bark, but I must go, and I am already going. I am her slave, no less than the women of her bedchamber. And to much the same end, it appears. She requires me to lie back upon the cushions, and she goes to dip both of her hands in the bowl of oil. I look up at her, at the luscious womanly curves I desire so much – and at the monster, standing erect from the juncture of her thighs, that she is slicking with one lazy hand. I cannot help wishing I had made it a little smaller.

'Lift your legs,' she tells me, grinning with anticipation.

I raise and open them, exposing the tight whorl of my sphincter. My cock lies across my belly like the trunk of a fallen cedar. 'This is wrong!' I snarl. 'Man was made greater and stronger than Woman, to have the mastery!'

'As were the Djinn made greater and stronger than us,' she says, running one slippery hand up my shaft, while probing for entry below with her cunning and well-lubricated fingers. 'And yet, who has the mastery there?'

I would argue, but I cannot speak. She is stroking my cock and the pleasure is exquisite, enough to transmute all the terror and shame of her other invasion to a delight almost its equal. I feel myself opening to her. She encompasses me at the same time as she enters me. The contradiction is acute, the confusion of my feelings unbearable – to be taken this way by a mortal, and a woman! – yet she is squeezing and pulling my limb in exactly the way I have needed for so long – oh, I do not understand this!

She leans over me and her bounteous breasts hang down like ripe and tantalising fruit. Her hands move with sureness and strength, and now my hole puts up no more resistance. Not even when her fingers make way for that unwomanly member and it pushes into me, as the footsoldiers of an army stand aside for the triumphal entry of their general into the conquered city.

'Oh,' she says in awe. 'That feels wonderful!'

I expect her to ravish me cruelly, but she does not lose control. Her conquest of my ass is thorough and measured. She leaves no inch unplundered, yet she is merciful. Though beads of sweat spring out upon her breastbone, she keeps kneading my cock in her strong fingers, forcing me to own my pleasure. Her hand and her cock move in unison, until a groan is wrenched from my chest: a groan so deep that a roof-joist overhead cracks. I grab my knees with my hands and spread wider for her. Her face blurs over mine. I am losing the will to deny her. I am forgetting to hate. I want her cock inside me, deeper and deeper. I want her hands mastering my cock, forcing me to the bright and glorious moment of surrender.

That is when I come, spurting my quicksilver seed the whole length of my torso, roaring my release. The metallic liquid runs across my ribs and belly, evaporating in the desert air almost instantly. By the time I catch my breath there is nothing left. Only my ass carries on clenching rhythmically around her shaft.

Bilqis licks her lips. 'Most impressive,' she says huskily. Her face is flushed and her eyes bright, and I realise that she has not yet reached her own climax, even as she adds, 'But I fear that a woman's body is more to my taste.'

For a moment I misconstrue her meaning. 'Shall I change you back, mistress?'

'I mean, a woman's body *beneath mine*. Change, djinni.'

My eyes widen. 'Impossible!' I rasp.

'Nonsense. If you can get that big, brawny body down inside a lamp, you can change its shape in lesser ways. Do it.'

So I do. Burning with shame, I do. I become female, my bones and flesh flowing into new shapes; my waist narrowing, my hips flaring, breasts swelling to cushiony softness upon my chest. My cock vanishes. I lie before her as the most beautiful of djinniyahs, the colour of sky. Sensation chases over my whole body, every inch of my new skin thrilling with strangeness. My heart is pounding. No one has ever done this to me. No one has ever made me feel like this.

And all the time she stays balls-deep in my ass.

'Oh,' says she. '*Yes.*' To my amazement, that cock of hers – which I had already thought so hard and big – swells even further inside me. She stoops with a groan to mouth at my breasts; I discover that they are exquisitely sensitive. I have no length of my own any more, but she manages to get her hand into my open sex, caressing its slipperiness even as she starts to ram me deep and fast.

I realise quite suddenly that that part of me is teardrop-shaped – just like a lamp; with a deep well of oil and a burning flame at the tip.

My mistress rubs it, and I come at her command.

Katie
Angela Caperton

Katie bit Lionel's shoulder through the tweed jacket, his hand under her petticoat, on her thigh, igniting new sensations. Mary never told her about the tiny bubbles that filled her blood and muscles wherever he touched her. She pressed her hips against his, the proud bulge that filled so sweetly the hollow created by her lifted leg. He kissed her, urgent, his ardour more palpable than any cool kiss to the hand. Three days. It had only been three days, but Katie knew he was the one. They burned, they lined up so nicely. She freed his cock with knowing fingers, smeared the pearl of his desire over the head and guided him into her. An explosion of pleasure surged through her. This was life, this glorious acceptance of ecstasy and need.

This was all she had ever wanted.

This was what she had lived for.

* * *

Jenny fought to still her breath when she first met Dr William Loomis. Words formed on her lips, though they did not arise from her own will.

'It is my honour to meet you, doctor. I hope to repay your attentions with my ardour.'

Katie's voice. How strange to hear the spirit speak in a lighted room with no prayers, no music, no faith to summon her. Jenny braced herself for whatever might follow the uncommon manifestation.

Dr Loomis took Jenny's hand, his fingers firm and warm. She thought at first he meant to kiss it, but instead he found her pulse and measured her with his touch.

'Your heart is beating very fast, Miss Sullivan,' he said.

Again, it was not Jenny who answered him, but Katie's teasing tone. 'I am eager to show you all that I can do.'

Dr Loomis exchanged a significant look with Uncle Hughie. 'I suppose, if you do not object to remaining awhile, Morton, we can run a test or two.'

'Here?' Uncle Hughie indicated the doctor's drawing room, warmly lit by gas lamps and the filtered sunlight of afternoon.

'Of course not. In the examining room.'

'For a full materialisation, a cabinet is best.'

'We won't attempt anything so grand today, Morton,

but, if Miss Sullivan has something to show me, I would hardly be a gentleman if I refused.'

'I beg your pardon, doctor.' Jenny's cheeks burned with embarrassment. Her words rushed out with truth and an invitation to believe. 'It wasn't me that offered. It was Katie.'

'Indeed?' Dr Loomis pressed the back of his hand to her forehead. Heat bloomed between them like wax under a seal. 'I do not believe you are feverish. You truly mean it was your spirit girl who spoke to me just now?'

'It was my spirit guide, doctor. No other, and, although I wish to cooperate with you in every way, I am not nearly so bold as Katie. You need to know that.' She wondered if he had heard any of the scandalous stories. More than once, Katie had planted harlot's kisses on someone in the séance circle. A few times she had even dared worse.

Mr Hugh Morton – Uncle Hughie, as many in the spiritualist church called him – had arranged this meeting. Hugh Morton was leader of the church, president of the Psychical Research League, a friend of young Dr William Loomis and a major contributor to the downtown paupers' clinic where Dr Loomis volunteered. 'If Dr Loomis vouches for your abilities, Jenny,' Uncle Hughie had entreated, 'we can convert a multitude of needy souls to the church.'

'But what if I can't?' she had asked, disappointed in herself as she pulled at her lace collar. 'It will not be the same in his cold chamber, the way it is in someone's parlour or the church. What if Katie will not come?'

But now, as Dr Loomis led her from the drawing room and into his examining room, Jenny felt Katie's legs inside her own, the press of Katie's breasts behind the stays of her corset, Katie's rose-scented breath in her nostrils.

Katie would come. Jenny had no doubt of that now. But please God, make her behave.

'Shall I disrobe?' Again Jenny's mouth formed the sounds, but Katie's voice controlled them. Jenny wished that they were Katie's cheeks burning hot with shame, not her own.

'No need this time, my dear,' Dr Loomis said. 'This won't be a controlled test. Not a test at all, really. Sit there.' He pointed to a chair like a barber's seat that could be made to recline. She settled into it, gathering her skirts modestly. Uncle Hughie stood against the plain wall while Dr Loomis stood beside Jenny. He looked into her eyes, and continued to hold her hand.

The doctor rose above her, like a handsome young god, strong-jawed with a trim moustache and steel-coloured eyes behind black-rimmed spectacles that did not diminish his virile aura one little bit. She wanted more than ever to make him a believer.

The mesmeric force of his gaze stroked her skin, her blood, unconscious but powerful, and she felt Katie's face filling her own, ethereal flesh pushing past the thin wall between this world and the next.

'Who am I speaking to now?' Dr Loomis asked.

'Katie.'

'Where are you, Katie?'

'I am here now, in the world of sorrows.'

'Where were you before?'

'Before when, William?'

'Before you began to speak.'

'I am always with Jenny, but I was also in the Summerland.'

'Ah yes. And before you were in the Summerland?'

'I lived in Tarrytown. I was a seamstress.'

'What year was that?'

'I left in 1832, when I was twenty years old. I caught a grippe and died in a week.'

Uncle Hughie spoke behind the doctor. 'We have of course verified that a young woman named Katie Green died of disease in Tarrytown in that year, but I fear we know little else about her.'

'I led a quiet life,' Katie said and Jenny ached with Katie's wistfulness. 'I left almost nothing behind me save a gravestone.'

'Why are you here now? Why do you manifest yourself in Miss Sullivan?' As he asked the question, Dr Loomis disengaged his fingers and took a stethoscope from the little table beside the chair.

Katie shifted to accommodate him as he pressed the horn trumpet of the instrument between the buttons of her blouse. Dissatisfied, he unfastened her bodice for better access and she felt the warmth of his fingers, though his manner was cool and professional, as he listened to Jenny's beating heart and to her breath.

'I am here to tell you there is life after death, William, but more than that I am here to teach you that life must be lived with fullness. Poor Jenny needs my lessons most of all.' Katie rested Jenny's hand atop Dr Loomis's, pressing the tips of his fingers against the swell of her bosom.

'A curious lesson,' Dr Loomis said, making notes. Jenny didn't miss the look that passed between him and Uncle Hughie.

'She is here to prove the teachings of the spiritualist church, doctor,' Uncle Hughie said. 'You may examine her as we agreed and then we can discuss your endorsement.'

'In time,' Loomis said, his gaze heavenward as he listened to Jenny's chest. 'Your faith in the afterlife is not the only possible explanation for these phenomena, Mr Morton. I have a colleague who believes that all "spirits" are actually projections of the medium's own brain. He cannot be with me for these experiments, but his hypothesis will not be ignored.' He looked at Jenny. 'Will you return this Friday, Katie? In the afternoon?' He drew his hand and the stethoscope away, Katie's grip resisting a little at first, then relaxing and allowing Jenny's hand to fall limply into her lap.

Breathless – for she was confined tightly by the stays

of Jenny's corset, even though her dress had been half undone – Katie answered. 'Oh, I will come, William,' she said. 'And you may examine me as much as you wish. I will give you satisfaction.' Then the spirit laughed wickedly, and Jenny's face burned red as boiled beets, even as she found her own voice again.

'Yes, Dr Loomis,' she said, the words trembling. 'I will be here. *We* will, I mean.'

* * *

On Friday, Jenny, Uncle Hughie and the intimidating bulk of Mrs MacDonnell rode in the most elegant hansom Jenny had ever seen, sent personally by Dr Loomis to fetch them.

Uncle Hughie rested his hand on her knee and squeezed reassuringly. 'I don't need to tell you how much is at stake today, my dear,' he said.

Jenny knew the stakes all too well. She had thought of little else since her first session with the professor. She wished earnestly that she could talk things over with Katie, if only to tell the impertinent, reckless spirit that she must not compromise Dr Loomis's principles, but any time Katie came, Jenny could not talk to her. They shared senses and even some thoughts, but conversation had never been possible between them.

'She knows, Hughie. Don't make her more nervous

than she already is.' Meg MacDonnell, Jenny's chaperone and a matron bigger than most men, winked at her. Meg was usually present any time Jenny disrobed during a séance, though Jenny felt Meg had allowed certain wealthy sitters to be too bold before she pushed her round belly and big bosom in front of Jenny to stop potential trouble. Uncle Hughie often reassured Jenny that delay was sometimes necessary, because interrupting the séance could be dangerous. Caution must be exercised, even at the risk of Jenny's chastity.

Jenny half-wished Meg had not come, but she knew that Dr Loomis would insist on a female guardian for the sake of propriety, and Meg was better than a stranger.

The cab deposited the three at Dr Loomis's brownstone building, where a butler admitted them into the doctor's study. Dr Loomis greeted them with a warm smile that tickled Jenny's belly.

'We will conduct the experiment here,' he pronounced, pumping Uncle Hughie's hand and bowing politely to Meg before he offered his arm to Jenny. 'But we will begin in the examining room. Do not be frightened, my dear. I have seen many women in an unclad state. You must undress completely. Remove everything, even your jewellery.'

She followed him, her heart pounding, not only at the thought of disrobing before the doctor but at the sudden imminence within her skin. She felt Katie waiting impatiently, a tigress ready to shred the material threshold.

Uncle Hughie and Meg followed them. The examining room seemed quite crowded when they all gathered within.

Uncle Hughie looked around the little room. 'Do you have a cabinet, doctor?'

'Not today. We will see how these tests go and, if I am satisfied, next time we will attempt a materialisation.'

Jenny knew Uncle Hughie would be disappointed. He had emphasised the importance of summoning Katie's spirit form as absolute proof of the survival of the lost woman's soul. The spirit had never emerged fully except in those séances when Jenny had been shut inside a standing cabinet to conceal the ectoplasmic extrusions from the circle's eyes. She sagged at the thought that this day might prove a failure.

Uncle Hughie and the doctor turned their heads away while Jenny removed her clothing. She thanked her foresight in dressing lightly, leaving the corset and petticoats at home, so it did not take her long to bare herself except for a flimsy shift. When Dr Loomis turned his attention on her again, she drew the thin garment over her head. The room's heat warmed her flesh.

She savoured the equal heat of Dr Loomis's eyes for a moment before he seemed to master his emotions and appraise her with an even, businesslike demeanour.

'Ah,' he said, gesturing at her mouth and throat. She obeyed him, opening wide and watched through slatted eyes as he examined her throat, her palette, and lifted her tongue with his fingers to touch with delicate ease the intimate spaces of her mouth. Then he unbound her hair, tossed the ribbon aside and let the wavy gold run between his fingers as he probed and stroked her scalp until he had touched every strand.

To Jenny's mortification, Katie bloomed under her skin, eager for what must come next.

Uncle Hughie watched furtively over Dr Loomis's shoulder and Meg stared openly as the doctor helped Jenny up onto the table. He spread her bare thighs and rested his warm fingertips against the lips of her sex. Jenny opened to him as he gently probed, but she flinched a little when he touched her maidenhead. Inwardly she cringed as Katie whispered mischievously, 'Will you help with that, William?'

Dr Loomis drew back, surprise on his face, but then he calmed, his quest for knowledge trumping any shock or curiosity he might feel about her virtue. He withdrew his fingers from her. 'Katie?'

Jenny shook her head. 'Not now,' she answered. 'But she is close.'

The doctor drew a deep breath and helped Jenny roll onto her stomach. Moist, slick fingers pressed against her backside, then into her. She had never been touched

48

there before – no other investigator had been so thorough – and the sensation surprised her, more pleasant than she would have expected. Katie bloomed again, this time pressing her bottom up against the doctor's hand. When the doctor allowed Jenny to roll over and sit up, she saw that his face burned red.

He finished his examination, concentrating on her hands and feet, then offered her a white robe. 'Dress, Jenny. Depending on the nature of our results, I may ask you to remove it again.'

Jenny reached for the robe, but Katie received it and tossed it aside. 'Like this,' Katie said, rising from the table bare as Venus. 'I'd rather we do it like this.'

Dr Loomis picked up the robe, looked at Uncle Hughie and at Meg, and then nodded. 'Very well. Let us return to the study.' He offered his arm again and Katie took it. She savoured her bare breast brushing against his upper arm, the friction causing her nipple to become stiff. Jenny grew noticeably moist between her legs with each step. This was Katie's fault and Jenny feared for what lay ahead.

'Perhaps,' she began as they entered the study, where the gas had already been turned low, the light like that of guttering candles. 'Perhaps we should …'

Dr Loomis led her to a small, sturdy chair, leather upholstered and utilitarian in its design. 'Yes?' he said. 'You want the robe?' He offered it to her again.

Katie shook Jenny's head as she sat down. Katie then

whispered right in the doctor's ear, 'No, I wished to say perhaps we should do this alone.'

Jenny saw the shock in his eyes, for her fleshly lips were far from his head and yet she knew the professor had just heard Katie's voice, so close he might have felt breath had there been breath to feel. Then Katie kissed his cheek with invisible lips, warm with life, though no eye could see them.

'Remarkable,' William Loomis said as he touched his cheek. 'Was that you, Katie?'

A rapping commenced near the top of the study's wainscoting and moved around the room as though an impossibly tall figure were tapping within the wall. The gaslights flickered and one of them went out. 'Turn it off, Morton,' Dr Loomis commanded as he knelt by Jenny's chair while Uncle Hughie adjusted the gas jet.

'We cannot do this alone,' he said. 'For no one would believe me if we do not have witnesses.'

Katie laughed and the rapping grew wilder, a volley of taps and drumming, before the room fell silent. 'You mean no one would believe you kept your trousers on, Willie,' she said to him. 'I know you're hard for me. I can feel you.'

Dr Loomis jumped and Jenny knew that Katie had touched him in an intimate place and she knew, as though she too had touched him, that Dr Loomis was rigid with lust.

'How did you cause that commotion, Katie?' he said,

trying to keep his tone level. 'How can you reach so very high?'

'I am not bound as you are,' she said. The buttons at the fly of the doctor's pants began to pop. Another light flickered out.

'Stop that,' he commanded, and Katie laughed with Jenny's lips, but she stopped her mischief. A bit of white cotton shone through the breach in his trousers, but Dr Loomis did not bother to adjust himself. His hair looked mussed and a bead of sweat teetered on his furrowed brow. 'Were you a wicked girl when you lived?' he asked.

'I was happy … once,' she said. 'Some might call it wicked. I didn't.'

'Is there no hell that punishes wickedness?'

'Hell there may be, but I have not seen it, nor have any here.'

'Here? In the Summerland?'

'No, silly Willie. In this world.' Another flurry of raps resounded around the room.

'You are no longer afraid of what wickedness might bring?'

Jenny's blood slowed in her veins even as her pulse grew deep. She knew the abyss would open soon, that Katie would emerge fully and that all that followed would be like a dream, if she remembered it at all. She did not want to go. She wanted desperately to see what Katie did with this handsome doctor, to know his hands on her body again,

51

to probe that exposed white cotton with her own hand. At the edge of the precipice, she blushed crimson with desire.

'There are worse things than wickedness, sweet William. To pass cold and unknown from the world, to deny the purpose for which our flesh was created, to resist love.'

'Dr Loomis,' Morton stepped forward, his gaze devouring Jenny's exposed skin. 'Surely now you believe in the return of souls?'

Dr Loomis turned to him, his warm hand resting on Jenny's shoulder. 'I have hardly seen enough, my good man, to convince me of any such thing as the return of the dead. There is something to this business surely, but as a scientist I must not draw too hasty a conclusion.'

'But the physical phenomena?'

'They prove nothing of the spiritual, Mr Morton. I believe in things I can see and weigh, but I also know the mysteries of the human brain are almost entirely unknown to us.'

Although Jenny's head did not move, Katie extended her invisible long tongue and licked the web of flesh between the doctor's thumb and forefinger. Jenny felt Katie's sentiment rising like urgent floodwaters, her anger growing as the men spoke about her as though she were a beaker boiling above a Bunsen burner.

Uncle Hughie's voice dropped a little and took on a conspiratorial tone. 'If you wish, doctor, Mrs MacDonnell and I can leave you here so that the examination may proceed undisturbed?'

'Oh, you'll leave all right,' Katie spat, the voice coming from within Jenny's bosom but deeper, echoing out of the well of time and space. 'And I will show the doctor all I can do. Not for your church or for his science, but for my own desire. Don't think to deny me now.'

A breeze rose within the confined space of the room, fluttering the notebooks and letters to become the north wind of autumn. The last gaslights flickered. Jenny peered out of her own skull as though through a veil. Katie had grown beyond her skin to fill the room. Uncle Hughie and Meg both looked stricken as Katie began to punch and poke them, almost playfully at first, then hard enough to bring red marks when she slapped their faces, the blows sharp, ringing above the thunder and rattle of the rapping that filled the chamber, every surface a drum for invisible hands.

Dr Loomis stood stupefied and watched as the two spiritualists were driven from the room, the knocking and pounding chasing them into the entry hall and probably out of the house. The study door slammed behind them. Then the noise faded, dying out until it became only the natural settling of a room, the walls and beams popping as with a change in temperature or the force of a storm against the timbers of the house.

One of Dr Loomis's servants knocked on the door, which appeared bolted from the inside.

'All is well. Leave me be,' the doctor called out, his tone steady and sure. In the dim light, his gaze, when he looked back at Jenny, shimmered with wonder and no trace of fear. She saw lust there too and shared Katie's delight in it.

Katie drew her shoulders back, thrusting her breasts out boldly. 'Touch me, Willie,' she said. 'Weigh me in your hands.'

He obeyed her, his touch less professional now, the caress of a man upon a woman.

'Are you Katie?' he asked, his voice husky. 'Or are you Jenny?' He leaned to kiss her before she might answer. She pressed against the hard muscle of his chest and welcomed the heat of his lips on hers.

His hands wandered, exploring and measuring, but not in the manner of a doctor. Their joined breath quickened in the fire that grew between them. He removed his shirt and Jenny touched his chest, his shoulders, her fingers gentle while Katie's hands scratched and pulled. Together they finished unbuttoning the doctor's trousers and freed his glorious instrument.

Jenny had never seen a man naked before and she had never imagined that one could be so beautiful as the doctor. Lost in his kisses and the attentions of his strong hands, she felt Katie entwine with both of them. Jenny shivered at the slipping of flesh when Katie emerged, but fought hard to hold onto her presence in the here and now. She didn't resist Katie, didn't try to shove her away, but only fought for her own place within the circle of the doctor's arms.

Dr Loomis sucked in air, surprised when Katie's hands caressed his back. Jenny's skin tingled with the shared sensations. Another torso, warm as living skin, pressed against hers, breasts and hips, thighs that sandwiched his, even as he entered Jenny, his shaft penetrating easily and wondrously, the moment of breach sharp and lovely as a thorn upon a perfect rose.

With Katie's hands joining Jenny's, they pulled and kneaded the hard muscles of the doctor's back and buttocks as he moved with feverish skill. Jenny's hips moved with him, her substance diminished by what Katie had borrowed from her, but all her senses ablaze and alive, the pleasure deep and true as anything she had ever known, the climax divine, expanding through her senses, bright as dawn.

Jenny heard the doctor utter a cry and knew he must have opened his eyes to see Katie, fully formed and tangled with them, radiant as though she were alive.

'I am going mad,' the doctor said. 'Divinely mad.' He looked into Jenny's eyes, his gaze probing hers, brave and open. 'What are you? What is she?'

Jenny shook her head and Katie answered for both of them. 'I am your muse, Willie. A goddess if you will, or a woman if you'd rather. I am all the things you cannot know save by your faith, all the delights you cannot measure. Hold me and I will give you wonders.'

Dr Loomis held her then, hard and close, his breathing deep, overwhelmed, and Jenny knew they would be happy for ever.

She and William.

And Katie.

Sleepwalker's Secret
Rose de Fer

Martin stepped out into the chilly night, closing the door of the Moon and Sixpence behind him. From within he could still hear the crack of snooker balls, the shouts from the rowdy group watching a match in the corner, gales of laughter from the hen party by the window. Everyone was having a great time except him and their joy felt like mockery. His stomach rumbled, unimpressed by what little he'd eaten of his burger and chips. The food hadn't been up to the pub's usual standard. Neither had the beer he'd barely touched. But then, everything probably would have been fine if he hadn't been stood up.

He was still smarting from the shame of the wasted evening and the painful sense that everyone there was laughing at him. Or worse – pitying the lonely bloke sitting in a corner by himself, checking his watch and his phone every couple of minutes and glancing up at the door. Why had Carol said yes in the first place if she wasn't interested in him? She was the first girl he'd had the courage to ask out in months. He shrugged into his coat and headed for the darkened car park at the rear of the building.

As he passed a small alley on his right he thought he heard a voice and he stopped to listen. A few moments later it came again, a low unhappy moan. Probably just some poor bastard who's had too much to drink, he thought. He was about to continue on his way when he heard it again and realised that the voice was female. His protective instincts triggered, he ventured into the mouth of the alley.

'Hello?' he called. 'Is someone there?'

The woman moaned again and there was the rustle of paper as she struggled to her feet. She was backlit by a streetlamp at the other end of the alley and he realised with a jolt that she was stark naked. He froze, staring at her shapely silhouette for several seconds before finally getting hold of himself and the situation.

'Oh my God,' he blurted out. He immediately stripped off his coat as he hurried towards her. 'Are you OK?'

A tiny voice at the back of his mind tried to warn him that this might all be a trap, that a chivalrous male was the perfect mark. But surely there were better and more reliable ruses than the sight that greeted him now.

She was not only naked but filthy. Her arms hung

limp at her sides and her long blond hair was tangled with leaves and twigs. Every inch of her was streaked with mud. At least he hoped it was mud.

'Are you hurt?' he asked cautiously. As he wrapped his coat around her shoulders he also noticed that several of her fingernails were broken off. He winced, instantly imagining the worst. The girl clasped the edges of his coat and blinked up at him slowly, uncomprehendingly. Beneath the muck, she was strikingly pretty. Vivid green eyes shone from under ropes of muddy hair. She didn't seem to know where she was.

'Come on,' Martin said. 'We should call the police and get you to a hospital.'

Her confusion seemed to clear somewhat at the mention of the police and she shook her head fiercely. 'No,' she said, her voice low and hoarse.

'But you've been attacked!'

'No police.'

'Well, a doctor, then. You need help, love.'

She closed her eyes and shook her head again. Took a deep breath. 'No.'

Martin didn't know what to do. Did 'no' mean she didn't *need* help? Or just didn't *want* it? He couldn't be sure of anything any more. Earlier that day he'd assumed that 'yes' meant a girl was interested in him. Now it seemed he had reason to doubt everything.

She peered around, taking in her surroundings. The

alley, the newspapers and damp cardboard boxes at her feet. Her broken and bloodied nails. She mumbled something that sounded like 'Not again' before her legs trembled and she lost her balance. An empty beer bottle went rattling against the brick wall and smashed.

Martin caught her before she could fall or step in the broken glass. 'Look, I can't just leave you here,' he pleaded, 'but, if you won't let me call someone, what can I do?'

She offered him a weak smile and pressed up close to him, resting her head against his chest. 'Home,' she murmured.

'OK, yes, I can take you home. Where do you live?'

But she shook her head again. 'No. *Your* home.'

Martin started to protest but the girl curled more tightly into his chest and he felt her trembling from the cold. His heart twisted. Even though she smelled like a wet dog she was still a beautiful young woman in need of help. And he'd always been a sucker for a damsel in distress. There was nothing to do but take her with him. Whatever had happened to her, she clearly didn't want the authorities involved. He could see no reason for that unless she'd been involved in something criminal. In which case his getting involved with *her* was a very bad idea indeed. But he couldn't just leave her there. If she didn't freeze to death someone else might find her. Someone without Martin's sense of gallantry.

Fine, then. He would take her home, make her a cup of tea and get her to tell him what had happened. Then maybe she'd be ready to call the police. Where was the harm in that?

'OK,' he said, not entirely reluctantly. 'Home.'

She said nothing on the short drive to his flat and he found himself chattering inanely to fill the awkward silence. He told her all about his disappointing evening and he even told her how much he still missed his best mate, who'd got a job in Canada and moved away a few months before. With no friends or family nearby, he felt isolated and cut off. He knew he must sound desperately lonely, but it felt good to talk to someone, even if he wasn't sure she understood.

Soon they reached the unremarkable building where he lived and he led her upstairs to his flat. It was small and cramped, even for one, but at least it was clean. He ducked into the bedroom to fetch his dressing gown for her. She glanced at it but didn't take it.

'I'm fine,' she said. She seemed completely oblivious to the fact that she was naked but for his coat.

'Well, you'll at least want to clean up,' he offered, gesturing towards the bathroom. 'You can wash the mud off and I'll make you a drink.'

She glanced down at herself and only then seemed to understand. But instead of shock or horror, the expression on her face was one of amusement. She shook her

61

head and grinned up at him, her green eyes gleaming like emeralds. 'Oh dear,' she said. 'I am in a bit of a state.'

Martin frowned, disturbed by her nonchalance. 'You haven't – erm, hit your head or anything, have you?'

Incredibly, she laughed. 'No, no, it's nothing like that, I assure you.' She chewed her lip for a moment, thinking. Then she said, 'I sleepwalk.'

It was such a simple and innocent explanation and it immediately wiped away all the terrible scenarios Martin had been envisioning. It cleared up everything. He heaved a huge sigh of relief. 'Oh, thank God for that,' he said. 'You really had me worried.'

'Sorry. I must have got as far as the woods this time and then lost my way coming back.'

'No wonder you didn't want me to call the police,' Martin said with a laugh. He felt like an enormous weight had been lifted from his chest. 'Here, I'll run you a bath and put the kettle on.'

The girl smiled. 'You're very kind,' she said. 'And I'm sorry again if I made you worry needlessly. I was ... a bit out of it.'

'You're no trouble at all,' Martin reassured her. Then he had to stop himself lest he get carried away. Already her eyes were proving hypnotic and it was all he could do not to stare at anything else, particularly the swell of her bare muddied breasts. His trousers were beginning to feel tight and he forced himself to turn away.

In the bathroom he sent a torrent of hot water into the tub and tried not to imagine her sinking blissfully into it.

'There you go,' he said, his tone one of forced casualness. 'Take as long as you need. I've put some clean towels out for you.'

'You're very generous,' she said. 'My name's Mia, by the way.'

Although he tried not to stare at her, something in her sultry tone made it impossible. He mumbled his own name back and then swallowed hard as his eyes travelled from her feet, up her long legs, to the smooth delta at their apex. As he watched, she parted her thighs slightly, just enough to give him a glimpse of the sleek folds nestled there.

Martin felt a hot blush spread over his face and throat, but several seconds passed before he was able to make himself look away. It was as though she had bewitched him. When his eyes at last found hers again, she was smiling.

* * *

Mia sank into the steaming water and lay back, closing her eyes. She could still taste the blood, still feel the adrenalin pumping through her body as she chased the rabbit into the depths of the forest and finally caught it. The moon shone through the trees in eerie blue rays and she followed the light deep into the undergrowth. She kept to the outskirts of the city, wary of the noise of traffic and people. Such things had vague resonance for her, but in her animal state she knew them only as threats.

As a wolf she experienced a kind of freedom no human ever could. A sense of oneness and connection to the world and its primal rhythms. She felt no shame, no guilt, no artifice. None of the troublesome emotions that defined life as a person. It was a state of pure honesty, of pure *being*.

The change only came at night, but it didn't always last until morning. She'd had to abandon her own flat in the city years ago in favour of a lonely cottage on the edge of the woods. It made her feel like the ostracised old woman in some mediaeval village, feared and shunned by the peasants who could so easily be rallied into a torch-wielding mob. But it was simply too dangerous to risk coming out of a transformation where people might see her. Or worse – where she might harm them.

She'd been incredibly lucky this time. She didn't want to think about what might have happened if she'd been found by the police. Changing back always left her dazed and a little amnesiac about where she'd been and what she'd done, but the memories soon returned. There was also an obscure feeling of sadness, a mourning for the wilder half of her double life. The wolf died each time she returned to normal.

She splashed herself half-heartedly with water and frowned at her broken fingernails. One time she had been shot at by a farmer and she had a scar from where the bullet had grazed her left leg. It was a dangerous existence but she wouldn't forsake the wolf for anything. Human relationships were messy, complicated affairs. The wolf knew no such awkwardness. She was the best part of Mia, the purest part.

'Everything all right in there?'

Martin's voice startled her from her reverie and she smiled.

'I'm fine,' she called back.

Her skin tingled at the thought of him, at the wave of lust she'd felt as he sacrificed his coat for her and gently helped her into the car. Another solitary soul like her, she mused. The wolfish urgency and instinct had filled her with desire and she had been unable to resist teasing him with her nakedness, flaunting her sex. The primal freedom of the wolf was the most potent aphrodisiac.

'But I feel a little dizzy,' she suddenly heard herself add in a tremulous voice. 'Could you maybe … help me?'

She grinned at the weighty silence that followed. She knew he was just on the other side of the door and she knew he was just as hungry as she was. She had to have him before the wolf faded completely.

Slowly the door opened and he peeked inside, trying not to look at her nakedness and failing. She saw the sympathy in his face as he took in her filthy state again. She hadn't made any effort to clean herself.

'You poor thing,' he said, kneeling beside the bathtub.

Mia met his compassion with a seductive little pout and held up one arm. Martin plucked a sponge from the edge of the tub and dunked it in the water. Then he drew it along her arm, scrubbing gently at the mud. She moaned with pleasure, closing her eyes and lying back in the tub, making it easier for him to look at her.

The musky scent of his arousal teased her as he washed first one arm, then the other. Sudsy water slid over her skin, tickling and stimulating her. At her soft intake of breath he stopped. She opened her eyes.

'Your face,' he said, his voice husky with barely concealed need.

She sat up, smiling sweetly at him as she tilted her head back. The action forced her back to arch, pushing her breasts forward. She felt her nipples stiffen as they were exposed to the air and she kept her eyes closed, inviting him to appreciate the sight.

She knew she was pretty. She also knew that her wolf blood gave her a special kind of allure. There was something feral about her that he wouldn't be able to pinpoint but would still respond to. Men could sense the beast within her. Many were frightened or intimidated by it, if not simply put off by her forthright nature. But Martin was aroused by it.

He was so open and trusting, so beautiful. She found herself staring at his deep-brown eyes as he tried so hard not to meet hers. Would they widen with horror if he saw her truest self? Would they be tainted by fear at the sight of the untamed white wolf? Or would they shine with the same kindness and understanding she'd seen when he found her in the alley?

Martin soaked the sponge again and stroked it lightly over her cheeks and forehead, revealing the smooth pale skin beneath the mud. Water trickled into the tub and she heard his breathing over the tiny splashes. His hand trembled ever so slightly as his fingers brushed her face. Mia sighed and arched her back a little more before reaching up to guide his hand lower. She drew him down over her throat, along the ridge of her collarbone and down the line of her breastbone. Then with both hands she squeezed the sponge, sending a torrent of soapy water coursing over her breasts.

'Mmm, very nice,' she murmured, opening her eyes at last to meet his.

His eyes were wide with a kind of helpless expression she found utterly charming. His thoughts were transparent.

'You're not taking advantage of me,' she said teasingly.

When he continued to look conflicted she reached over and pressed her hand against the hardness that was straining inside his jeans. His eyes closed and he dropped the sponge into the water. Beneath her fingers she felt him grow even harder and after another second's hesitation he leaned forwards and mashed his lips to hers.

Mia returned the kiss, pushing her tongue deep inside his mouth, tangling it with his. She threw her wet arms around him and pressed herself against his chest, soaking him. His arms slid around her wet soapy body and he lifted her to her feet. Water streamed down her legs.

Martin broke the kiss at last, pulling away long enough to grab one of the towels he had laid out for her. He wrapped it around her and began gently patting her dry. Mia stood still, surrendering to the pleasure as he mopped the water from her skin and hair. She squirmed against the towel, urging him to rub her harder. Her skin was especially sensitive after a transformation and it responded sexually to any kind of stimulation, soft or hard, gentle or rough. And right now she wanted it rough.

When she was dry he gathered her in his arms and carried her through the doorway and down a short corridor. Mia nuzzled against his chest, enjoying the sensation of vulnerability. She'd had the night to feel powerful and wild; now it felt comforting to be tamed.

He laid her down on the unmade bed and she splayed her limbs wide for him, moving her hips sinuously as though dancing. He stared at her, spellbound by her animal allure. With trembling hands he unfastened his jeans and slid them down, only to find that he hadn't removed his shoes. Quickly he kicked them off and yanked his jeans down. Mia stared at the bulge in his underpants and gave a soft little moan of encouragement. In one fluid movement he had his shirt off and then, at last, he was on top of her.

She wrapped herself around him, pressing her sex against him, urging him wordlessly to take her. The head of his cock found the inviting wetness and probed gently for a moment before Mia drove herself onto him, impaling herself. Martin gasped as he plunged into the deep warm centre of her and she rocked her hips back and forth to show him the rhythm she liked. He bruised her mouth with kisses, devouring her like a starving man while she wrapped her legs around him and urged him deeper.

Her arms encircled him and without thinking she dug her broken fingernails into his back, clawing him hungrily. He hissed with pain through his teeth and broke away, staring at her with wide eyes, startled by her wildness. His sweet demeanour made her want to corrupt him and her lips curled in a wicked smile as she rolled them both to the side, flipping him onto his back with her astride him.

She couldn't help her nature. When the wolf in her wanted something, she took it. There was no meek, submissive request for what she wanted, no politeness or decorum. And yet she desperately wanted to be subdued, yearned to be conquered by someone who understood what drove her violent passions.

The night was still young and she felt the wolf stirring again within her, sensed the bloodlust and frenzy bubbling just beneath the surface. She wondered what he would do if she suddenly transformed.

His hands slid up her body and he cupped her breasts in his eager hands and Mia threw back her head as he tweaked her nipples. He bucked his hips beneath her, sending sparks of ecstasy through her entire body. When she leaned down to kiss him again he was more demanding, more forceful. He nipped at her lower lip and then bit down hard enough to make her yelp. She tasted blood.

Her eyes flew wide with delighted shock as he grew bolder, raking his fingernails down her back as she had done to him. She gasped, arching her body as his hands carved a path down either side of her spine. Her skin felt wildly alive with a delirious mix of pleasure and pain and suddenly he seized her and flipped her over onto her back. Her long hair was cool and wet beneath her scratched skin and she imagined him twisting it in his hand, pulling her head back as he fucked her from behind.

A wave of bliss surged through her as she surrendered to his control. Her flesh tingled with the wolf's craving for ferocity and dominance and she raised her arms up over her head, offering herself.

He got the message and immediately pinned her wrists down, his eyes wild with intensity. He was completely lost in the moment. First under her spell, then under his own. She thrashed beneath him as he pummelled her sex, driving himself in up to the hilt and then fully out again. Mia howled as she began to come, an unearthly wailing of pure animal joy. Her climax only excited him more and with a few more thrusts he soon reached his own orgasm, burying his face in her throat and crying out against her skin.

They lay panting and wrapped in each other's body for some time before Mia at last succumbed to the night's exertions. She drifted off to sleep in his arms like a trusting puppy.

* * *

Martin watched her as she slept. The soft rise and fall of her chest and her rhythmic breathing seemed completely at odds with the woman who had practically raped him the night before and then urged him to do the same to her. His body had never felt so aroused. It ached for more.

Mia had told him she was a sleepwalker, implying that somehow she'd managed to wander completely naked from her home and into the woods, where she could only have rolled in the mud like an animal to get so filthy. After this adventure, still asleep, she had then found her way back into the city, where she finally woke up – although not entirely – in an alley. Martin was certainly no expert on sleepwalking, but none of it rang true or made any kind of sense.

And that wasn't all. Something else strange was nagging at his mind. At one point during their mad passion Mia's eyes had seemed to change colour. No, that wasn't quite right; they had changed *shape* as well. The green irises had contracted to piercing black discs in slanted amber eyes. And when she'd thrown back her head with a wild cry, had her teeth really looked like fangs?

He shook his head. No, that was silly. He was obviously just drunk on the night's exertions. Drunk on *her*. His skin was still tingling from her touch, both tender and ferocious. It felt as though his blood was electrified, buzzing through his veins like a low-level current. A huge yawn overtook him as he finally began to succumb to his exhaustion and he had the bizarre thought that his teeth suddenly seemed too large for his mouth.

He wrapped his arms protectively around Mia, spooning her so she couldn't escape. She murmured contentedly and pressed back against him.

When he slept he dreamed of wolves, fierce beautiful wolves running through the forest and braving the streets and alleys of the city, free to roam wherever they chose. He had the oddest sense in the dream that at times he was one of them, one of the pack. The feeling made him sigh with pleasure in his sleep. He could almost taste the blood of the small creatures they hunted and killed. But most of all he felt a powerful bond with the sleek white wolf who ran by his side through the moonlit night.

When he woke several hours later, Mia had slipped from his grasp. He sat up, alarmed and dismayed at the thought that he might never be able to find her again. Then his panic melted into a smile as he saw her. She was sitting beside him on the bed, her paws crossed and her amber eyes shining in the moonlight that streamed in through the window. She swished her bushy white tail and licked his face.

They Come At Night
Elizabeth Coldwell

'I keep having this dream. Exactly the same, night after night.' Even as I said it, I shifted on the couch with embarrassment. It seemed such a lame thing to visit a therapist about, like I was taking time away from someone who could be lying here discussing a serious issue. Yet, to me, this *was* a serious issue; one that had been disrupting my sleep, leaving me feeling groggy in the mornings and unable to concentrate on doing my job, for months now.

Dr Fischer crossed a slim stockinged leg and reached for her notepad, regarding me with a look that made me feel this might not be a complete waste of time. If I was honest, what I needed more than anything was someone to listen to me. I'd exhausted all other options, from aromatherapy pillow sprays to heavy-duty sleeping pills prescribed by my doctor, and a sympathetic ear couldn't fail to go some of the way towards solving my problem, or so I hoped.

'Tell me about it,' she said.

'Where do I start?' I replied, half to myself.

'Well, how long have you been having the dream, for a start?'

'Just over six months now.'

I watched her scribble something on her pad.

'And what exactly is it about? Tell me in as much detail as you remember.'

Now, that I could do. Every last moment of the dream was burned on my memory, like someone had pressed a red-hot poker to a vital part of my brain.

Taking a deep breath, I began to describe the events that haunted me. 'I'm lying in my bed, and these two men come into the room. Big, powerful men. I never see their faces properly – they're always in shadow – but they have the most incredible bodies, like they're made of pure muscle, you know?'

Dr Fischer said nothing, just kept making notes in what looked like large, messy handwriting.

Not knowing whether to be encouraged by her silence, I continued. 'Anyway, these men, they – they pull back the covers, pin me to the bed and start ripping off my nightdress. It's almost like I'm paralysed, powerless to do anything to stop them. I should be afraid, but I'm not. Whatever they're going to do to me, I want it.'

'And what exactly is it that they do to you?'

Screwing my eyelids tight shut, I pictured them as

they appeared to me every night: dark eyes burning in their half-hidden faces, naked, sweat-slick flesh pressing hard against mine as they pawed at me. And I breathed the scent that clung to their bodies, a sharp mixture of male musk and something that could have been burned sandalwood. The scent seemed to linger in the air when I woke, making me feel what was happening to me was more than a dream, somehow, but, if I told Dr Fischer that, I knew she'd class me as delusional.

'Everything,' I replied at length. 'Their hands are all over me. One of them touches my breasts while the other runs his fingers lower, down between my legs. He strokes me there till I just can't stand it. I know they're both going to fu–' I managed to stop myself just in time. There are some words you really shouldn't use in a therapist's office, even if they might be the most appropriate in the circumstances. 'Make love to me. And they do. Over and over. They use my mouth, my vagina, my – well, you name it, they do it to me. And they're good. They're really, really good. They know just how to touch me, just where to lick to have me right on the point of coming, time after time. I know, when they finally let me come, it's going to be the most intense orgasm I've ever had in my life.'

I couldn't help noticing the way Dr Fischer shifted in her chair, crossing her legs as if she had a sudden itch in her pussy that needed to be scratched. If simply hearing the dream described was getting to her, how did she think I felt, experiencing it night after night?

'So what happens next?' she asked, the words tight in her throat.

I almost let out a small, bitter laugh. 'Next? They leave, of course, just as suddenly as they arrived. You see, by then they've had their fill for the night. And they don't care that, even though they've had as much pleasure as they can take, they still haven't satisfied me.'

Dr Fischer put her pen down. 'Well, Theresa, there's certainly a deal of frustration in your dream the way you describe it. Would you say you were under any stress at work?'

'No, I love my job.' It was true, even though it had been getting harder to drag myself the seven blocks from my apartment every morning and pin a smile on my face to deal with our more exacting customers, worn out as I was by this vivid, physically exhausting dream.

'What is it you do exactly?'

'I work at Santos and Salmon.'

'Oh, the deli over on West 10th? Yes, I know the place. I can see why you'd enjoy it there.' She fixed me with a questioning look. 'So work's fine. Which leaves one other area to explore, given the obviously erotic nature of your dream. And that's your sex life.'

'What sex life?' I hadn't had sex for more than nine months, not since I'd split up with Marty last Valentine's night. That had been the night I'd caught him fucking that brassy, fake-titted secretary of his over the desk in his corner office. Since then, I'd been resolutely single. At first, my friends had taken me out to the bars and nightclubs in the Village, hoping to hook me up with some eligible guy or other, but I'd failed to meet anyone I liked. Hell, most of the guys on the bar scene I struggled to hold a conversation with, let alone develop the urge to get closer to them, and as the months had gone past and the dream had gripped me ever tighter in its nightly grasp I'd gradually lost the will to socialise. 'I'm not even having a meaningful relationship with my vibrator any more,' I added.

'And so we get to the heart of the problem,' Dr Fischer said, underlining something she'd written while I'd been talking earlier. 'It seems to me this dream is nothing more than a literal manifestation of your sexual frustration.'

I pulled myself into a half-sitting position on the couch. 'So what you're saying is that, if I go out and get laid, the dream will stop?'

'Well, I wouldn't put it in quite such crude terms, Theresa, but, essentially, yes.' She glanced at the antique silver clock on her desk. 'And that's our time up. Would you like to schedule another session?'

I shook my head. 'Thanks, but that won't be necessary.'

As I stepped out into the crispness of that early December afternoon, striding away from Dr Fischer's office towards Central Park West, I felt a weight lift from my shoulders. Finally talking about the situation had made a difference, and maybe for the first time in months when I closed my eyes tonight I wouldn't be plagued by those two gorgeous but ruthlessly selfish dream lovers of mine.

* * *

That night, I spent a long time getting ready for bed, soaking in a lavender-scented bath before retiring to my bedroom with a big mug of hot chocolate, topped with cream and a handful of the cute mini-marshmallows we sold in the deli. When I'd got back to the apartment, a message had been waiting on the answerphone from one of my oldest friends, Judy. She was coming into Manhattan for a meeting tomorrow; maybe we could get together afterwards, go for a drink. It sounded like the perfect way to put Dr Fischer's suggestion into action. We could meet up at our favourite haunt, DeVito's, over on Delancey, for cocktails, and I intended to make sure I didn't leave there alone. There'd be clean sheets on my bed, a scented candle burning to welcome some lucky guy into my boudoir. For the first time in longer than I could recall, drifting off to sleep was an effortless act.

Some time in the middle of the night, I was half-woken by a scrabbling noise, like rats in the wainscoting. If I looked in the shadows, I was almost convinced I'd see something scurrying around. No rats here, I told myself firmly, but the sense of a presence in the room persisted. A scent rose to my nostrils, a familiar mixture of hot ash and exotic spice. How could that be? I'd convinced myself that smell existed only in my dreams, and I wasn't dreaming now.

Trying to bury myself deeper in the covers, I realised with a shock that I couldn't move as much as a finger. I knew exactly what this feeling of frozen helplessness preceded, at least while I slept, and so it came as no real surprise to see the two figures standing in the far corner, shrouded in darkness. This couldn't be happening; dreams were dreams, and this was – this was real. They strode forward in unison, and I could only watch as they came closer, unable to call out.

When the first of them pulled back the bedcovers and laid a hot, coarse-skinned hand on my chest, I found my body easing from its paralysis.

'What are you doing here?' I managed to croak, as he gripped the neck of my nightdress, tearing it down to the waist. 'Who are you?'

As I asked the question, a single word formed in the back of my brain, a relic of a long-ago history lesson. 'Incubus'. I could hear Mr Anderson, my tenth-grade history teacher, telling us about the Salem witch trials. Among all the hysteria, jealousy and accusation, the tale of the incubus – and its female equivalent, the succubus

– came up time and again in the written accounts of these trials. Sex demons, they came at night, praying on the chaste and virtuous. Some claimed they were conjured up from the depths of Hell, others that they were the witches themselves, changing their shape in order to seduce their chosen victim. All superstitious nonsense, Mr Anderson said, cooked up in mediaeval times as a way of avoiding any guilt about needing to be satisfied sexually, and explaining away such messy, incriminating things as nocturnal emissions.

'Do you mean wet dreams, sir?' Tommy Cocozza had chimed up from the back of the schoolroom.

'Indeed I do, Tommy,' Mr Anderson had replied, 'but of course you'd know all about those ...'

The lesson had dissolved in raucous laughter at his comment, any attempt at teaching us the finer points of seventeenth-century history lost for the day. I clung to the memory as my own nocturnal visitor stripped the last rags of the nightdress from me.

My limbs had recovered the ability to move, but I didn't try to shrink away from him. Somehow, he and his companion had stepped out of my dreams and into the quiet of my bedroom, and I should have been terrified. But I wasn't. As always, I knew what they intended to do to me, and I welcomed it.

A voice cut into my thoughts, a gravelled, seductive husk. 'We came because we know what you intend,' the incubus said, cupping my bare breast in one hand and letting his sharp-nailed thumb strum at my nipple. 'You want to find a mortal man to love you, to give you pleasure. But you are ours, Theresa, and you always will be. We mean to show you that tonight.'

I looked up, seeing his face clearly for the first time. High, prominent cheekbones, a long, hooked nose, lips set in a firm, sensual sneer. Beauty wrapped in a clear aura of danger. The eyes I was already familiar with; those dark chips of coal had haunted my nights for months now, seeming to see through to my very soul.

'Well, if that's the case, then tell me who you are.' My words dissolved into a moan as he pinched my nipple, sending a jolt of sheer erotic bliss down to my core. 'How can I be yours if I don't even know your names?'

'I am Astare,' he replied, 'and my brother is Balrok. But we answer to many names. Sir, Lord, Master ...'

Again that pressure on my puckered bud, mingling pleasure with pain. My pussy was hot, syrupy-wet, desire spiking sharp between my legs. I longed for Balrok to step forward and join his brother, but for the moment he seemed content to watch as Astare's other hand gripped my mound sharply. His fingers dabbled in the juice he found there, skimming the contours of my cunt lips and drawing another tortured moan from me.

'Is she ready for us?' Balrok asked, his voice carrying the same low, erotic quality as his brother's.

'Isn't she always?' Astare retorted. Then he leaned forward and did something he never had before. He laid a kiss on my lips, hard and forceful. A demon's kiss, designed to draw the breath – maybe even the life force – from me. I reached up, gripping fistfuls of his long black hair as I returned the kiss without hesitation. His tongue pushed deeper into my mouth, flickering in a way that made me think of reptiles and slithering things, but it didn't repulse me. I'd been in love with Marty for a long time – at least, I thought I had – but his kisses had never aroused the same passion in me as I felt right now. I'd never wanted him the way I wanted this strange, inhuman figure. What that would have told Dr Fischer about my mental state I neither knew nor cared.

Pushing me back against the mattress, Astare slid one thick, gnarled finger into my cunt, followed quickly by a second. Frigging me with a quick in-and-out motion, before bringing his thumb into the equation, rubbing at my clit, he soon had me writhing against the sheet. The ascent towards orgasm was a swift one, but he brought it to an abrupt halt by pulling his fingers away, leaving me empty and bereft.

'Come on, join me, brother.' He beckoned to Balrok, who still skulked in the corner. At his command, the second incubus stepped forward. A crack in the drapes allowed a shaft of cold neon light to fall into the room, and Balrok stood illuminated. Where the planes of his brother's face had drawn my gaze, it was Balrok's body that fascinated me. The ridges of muscle on his stomach were so taut and sculpted they would make the models on the men's fitness magazine covers weep with bitter envy, and his biceps and bulging forearms hinted at superhuman strength. But they were dwarfed by the beauty of his cock, rising up straight to his navel, so long even his two big hands wouldn't have covered the whole of it. I'd felt those unearthly dimensions in my pussy and arsehole on so many occasions as I dreamed, but they'd never truly registered with me until now. What happened while I slept was one thing, but was I really capable of taking so much thick, hard flesh without complaint?

Before I had time to fully consider the question, Balrok had joined his demonic brother on the bed. Between them, they manoeuvred me into their desired position, on all fours with my legs spread wide and my bare rump sticking out. This was how they liked to have me, mouth available to one and cunt or arse on display for the other to admire before fucking. I never knew which of them would take me in which hole first, but in the end it never seemed to matter. Before they left, they'd have enjoyed me everywhere, and my cream trickled down the insides of my thighs in anticipation. I shouldn't have wanted this as badly as I did, but having this pair of luscious incubi step from my fevered dreams and into reality made me hornier than I could have believed.

'So beautiful,' Astare murmured, his hand roaming down over the small of my back to caress each arse cheek in turn.

Now Balrok took the point of my chin in his hand and pressed his lips to mine. His kiss was as imperious as his brother's, taking my submission to him as a simple fact. While his tongue battled with mine, Astare's mouth latched on to my pouting pussy lips, pulling on them with a smacking, slurping sound that denoted pure relish.

Easing my cheeks wider apart, he buried his face deeper in my cunt, eating me out with a fierce hunger. Lost in the sweetness of the sensation, I broke away from Balrok's kiss to croon, 'Oh, God, that's it! Keep doing that. Lick my cunt. Lick my arse, master ...'

I'd never been one for talking dirty in bed, but Astare's wicked tongue tricks were taking me to a place where I barely recognised myself. When Balrok caught my nipple between his lips and sucked hard at the same time as his brother laved my clit, the twin onslaught of pleasure made me groan.

Their pervasive, spicy smell was strong in the room, mingled with the briny aroma of my thickly flowing juices. Somewhere, a little voice warned me that I was in way over my head. Consorting with demons couldn't end well. But, I reasoned, they could only take from me what I was prepared to give. Dr Fischer had laid my life out neatly as we discussed my problem in her office: just another lowly shop girl, albeit with an enviable position on the staff of a high-end deli, in need of some excitement and fulfilment in her humdrum life. Now here were two stupendously put-together creatures of the night offering me all that, and more. And if there were consequences – well, I'd deal with those later.

Astare's tongue swiped over the tight furl of my arsehole, the wet, illicit caress causing me to squirm back against him. None of my human lovers had ever licked me there, and, as the point of Astare's tongue poked more insistently at my rear hole, I knew just how much pleasure I'd been missing out on.

In front of me, Balrok was gripping his monstrous cock in his fist, urging me to open my mouth wide and take him in. When I wrapped my lips around his crown, making him hiss between sharp, fanged teeth, I tasted salt, cumin and cloves. Nothing like I'd expected, but so appetising that I lapped at the hot virile flesh with abandon.

While I was busily occupied sucking Balrok, Astare guided his cockhead between my pussy lips. As he sought entry, I wondered how I could ever accommodate something so freakishly big. But he kept on pushing till my walls relaxed and he slid inside, stretching me so wide my whole cunt seemed to quiver. My clit stood out, raised and prominent, and I knew the slightest touch there would send ripples of almost unbearable pleasure through the lower half of my body.

Balrok fed more of his cock down my throat, plugging it just as securely as his brother had plugged my pussy. He gave me a moment to adjust to this state of almost obscene fullness, no longer, before thrusting into my mouth in a slow, steady fucking motion. Beneath us, the bedsprings creaked as Astare started to move in a similar rhythm, every stroke pushing me on to Balrok's shaft. In that maddening recurring dream, this calculated spit-roasting had been good, but in reality it took me to a place beyond my wildest imaginings. Their ultimate pleasure might have been their chief concern, but, as they strove to bring themselves to orgasm, they were treating me to the ride of my life.

I lost all track of how long they fucked me for, their stamina beyond anything a mortal man could hope to match. They even took a break to switch positions, Astare replacing his brother in my mouth, while Balrok turned his attention to shafting my pussy, the change so swift and seamless I barely had time to mourn the loss of their cocks.

But even demons need to come eventually, and at last I felt the quickening in their thrusts and heard the frenzied gasping that let me know they were right at the edge.

'More,' I begged, pulling my mouth off Astare's cock. 'Don't stop fucking me, not yet.'

Astare gave a harsh laugh. 'Don't you realise you don't give the orders around here? You are ours,' he panted, struggling to form the words as his orgasm approached.

I shook my head and bit back a sigh, needing to assert

my desires. 'No. If I really was yours, then you'd care about my pleasure, both of you. You wouldn't just leave once you'd come. Demons or not, you'd make sure I had my satisfaction, too.'

Balrok paused in his thrusting, and I realised both of them were considering my words. Had it really not occurred to them until now that I might want to have my lust quenched by the two of them, to be taken to a place where I barely even knew who I was any more? It seemed I got my reply when his finger wormed its way between my trembling thighs, settling on my clit and moving in fast purposeful circles. The three of us moved in a renewed frenzy of lust, and I clutched at the crumpled bedsheet, pushed to the very limits of my endurance by my otherworldly lovers. Behind me, I felt Balrok stiffen, his cock pumping its seed deep into my belly. Spurred on by the sight of his brother's climax, Astare gave one final shove and loosed his load in the soft clutch of my throat. But they didn't pull away once they'd come, as they always had before, and Balrok's finger kept its steady pressure on my nub. The yawning chasm of my orgasm opened wide and swallowed me in.

As I came, body shaken by a climax more powerful than any I'd ever experienced, I knew that Astare had finally spoken the truth. If they could give me pleasure like this, nothing else mattered. At last, I was completely theirs. Tonight, tomorrow and for as many nights as they chose to visit me.

Period Drama
Lara Lancey

The interior of the house was pitch-black. This was how it would have been when it was originally built, in the days before electricity. All the plasterwork details on the walls and floors were edged out by the orange streetlight, which elbowed its way past her to stain the gloom inside. The front door creaked open like a horror movie to reveal a man who seemed at first as indistinct as the building around him. From where Fran was shuffling her feet on the worn stone doorstep, it looked as if he was floating a few inches above the floor.

'Rather awkward, I'm afraid, with no illumination.' He cleared his throat. His voice was rusty, as if he hadn't spoken for months. 'Perhaps you'd rather come back tomorrow, when there's more light. Can't see the detail on a dark evening like this.'

She shook her head with what she hoped was a

businesslike smile and stepped past him to come inside. He flattened himself back against the wall. The door groaned closed. The dusty air whispered into a little breeze, jostling and enveloping her. She should have been spooked, the way the shadows dragged at her, but instead they enticed her, like beckoning arms and fingers.

The curving stairs led her eyes upwards, daring her to explore the invisible upper storeys.

'Now I'm here,' she said, 'I'd like to look around.'

He dipped his head in a kind of salute, and shrugged one shoulder to gesture her through some double doors and into a cavernous room which smelled of wax and was bare except for a fire flickering at the far end. Three French windows opened onto ornate balconies above the oddly quiet street. Her shoes squeaked on the polished parquet flooring as she circled slowly.

'All the furniture has been removed. I've had to lurk up in the attic,' the man explained. 'Now I find it too heartbreaking to leave.'

Fran stopped twirling and glanced over her shoulder. He had stopped right behind her, hovering by the fire. There was an old mirror hanging there, so tarnished that the back of his head didn't show in the glass. The fluorescent lamplight from outside was dull as it tried to compete with the flames twisting sluggishly in the grate.

'You've been camping in the attic?' She thought she'd better make some kind of comment in the heavy silence.

She took a step nearer. It was freezing cold in the room, draughts snaking all round her shoulders, neck and ankles. She wanted to get closer to any warmth the fire might have to offer.

'Only place left for me.'

'Your office told me it was vacant possession. I arranged to meet an estate agent here at seven. I know I'm late but I had to rush home to change. I'm on my way to a soirée at the museum. They wanted us to come in historical costume so I've been to the hire shop –' Her voice petered out. 'Are you the estate agent?'

'I am Frederick Chalmers. This house is mine.'

His voice was stronger now and he rested his elbow elegantly on the mantelpiece like the aloof hero in a period drama.

'Perhaps I'm intruding, then,' Fran murmured, shivering quite violently now.

'People never stay long.'

The fire seemed to give off no heat whatsoever. 'I'm sorry. I didn't know the owner would be in residence. As I say, Mr James assured me it was vacant and that he had the keys. I expect he'll be here in a minute.'

'That's all right. I knew you were coming,' he interrupted, smiling. All she could see in the gloom was the flash of his teeth and a diamond of saliva on his lower lip. 'No inconvenience at all.'

'Good.' Despite the cold, she felt her mouth opening

in an answering smile. He was so still, like a statue, yet somehow not stony. Calming, like a balm. Her eyes felt scratchy and sore with the effort of peering through this half-light and being dazzled by the light from the fire.

'Well, you've restored it amazingly well.' She waved her arm around. 'I'm no expert, but I'm guessing early nineteenth century? Have you any candles? We could at least light it as it is supposed to be lit.'

'The year is 1800.'

Inclining his head in another odd sort of bow, he backed away and simply melted into the shadows. She liked the idea of secret doors and passages. Think of the tricks you could play at house parties!

She unbuttoned her heavy coat and as it dropped to the floor a cold draught whisked over the surfaces of her skin. Tiny hairs rose and prickled as the puffy sleeves of the Empire dress slipped off her shoulders. Her breasts were hoisted unnaturally high in the narrow bodice, resting on a row of stitching which gathered the fabric in to her ribcage and under her bosom. The lace framing them shook each time she took a breath, and they bulged against the tight seams.

The dress she had hired for tonight's party was the genuine article, right down to the yellowing buttons and snagged muslin. She had no idea if this was the costume of a lady or a servant girl, but how did those people move around, or relax? You could only move stiffly or swivel in tiny movements like a geisha. The effect was dainty and virginal, yet even the most boy-chested of women would have had their bosom thrust into people's faces like a Wonderbra model.

All she could focus on was those white mounds, how everyone at the party later would stare at them when she made her entrance, these puppies presented like pale melons in the embroidered bodice, and how soon it would be, if she sneezed or laughed or danced, before they lifted and overflowed from their constraints, the antique dress disintegrating round her with the sheer force and heat of her body bursting out of it.

People would crowd round, stare, maybe fondle or grab hold. Men would be unable to resist stepping forward and squeezing and nuzzling at her breasts. Women would blush at the sudden visible blackness of her pussy as the dress fell away. There would be a few fronds of muslin and lace left, clinging to the sweaty patches under her arms and inside her thighs, between her legs, then these would peel away like burning paper to leave her naked as Venus.

As she stood in the quiet house waiting for the guy to come back, her nipples started to burn, grazing the rough lining of the dress. There was no bra that would fit under this dress, and the chill in the room shrank them into sharp points. Only a scrap of shredded old lace between her nipples and the world.

She glanced at her watch. Shit. She must have taken it off when she tried the dress on. A clock was ticking ponderously somewhere in the house, but she didn't want to leave the feeble warmth of the fire. The orange streetlights had dimmed. There was only darkness to indicate the lateness of the hour. Damn it. She was going to be late.

But she couldn't move. Somehow she hadn't finished with this house. Or it hadn't finished with her.

She lifted the long dress and shuffled over to the mirror in the little satin slippers. Her reflection was clear in the dancing firelight. The ringlets she had quickly fashioned with her tongs earlier were still in place, twirling down on either side of her face. The rest of her hair she had knotted on top of her head, which elongated her white throat like a swan's, extending out of the swell of her breasts. Her make-up seemed to have faded, giving her a startled, innocent look. She looked like a publicity still for the latest Jane Austen drama. Demure, but oh so dirty.

'Not only candles, but I have wine here as well.'

The man was setting a silver tray and crystal decanter down on the floor. Her fingers played coyly over her lips, and her breasts rose higher out of the dress as she tried to steady her breathing.

'You must excuse my attire. It's for the party I told you about.' *Attire?* Since when had she started using words like that? His old-fashioned air was getting to her.

94

'Somehow the dress doesn't fit so well. It feels smaller than it did at the costumier.'

'The dress is just right for the occasion,' he answered, throwing some brocade cushions in front of the fire. He held out his hand to her. 'Now you belong here.'

'Perhaps just one glass, then. Women in those days didn't disport themselves in an unladylike fashion, did they?'

She grasped his ice-cold fingers to lower herself carefully on to the bed of cushions. Her limbs felt stiff, as if she had been holding her posture for too long, and instead of sprawling carelessly, she tucked her feet sideways under her and sat bolt upright, like a ballerina.

'Please. Drink,' he said, waving his arm at her. 'It's high time I had some company.'

She sipped from the heavy crystal and the wine felt treacly on her tongue, coating her throat as she swallowed. But it warmed her blood. She could feel the waves of intoxication lapping at her skull.

'There is no one here to see us now. No more intruders.'

He knelt down near her, and filled his own glass with the dark-red liquid. He examined her with his head on one side, like a devilishly attractive bird of prey. The stillness of his angular face seemed strangely mournful, though his eyes glittered black and restless. He had, after all, been roosting in the attic. His plumbing skills probably didn't extend to fixing the heat and hot-water systems in this rambling house.

So how come his shirt was so dazzlingly white? He must have been wearing a coat before, because now she noticed the shirt and the way it was loosely open over his chest and ruffled over the buttons and cuffs. His long legs were encased in tight breeches and a bubble of amusement rose in her throat to see that he was wearing leather riding boots.

'This is extraordinary!' she choked, swishing her glass wildly as she covered her mouth with her other hand. 'The clothes you're wearing! You must be going to the same function as me.'

He drew a large handkerchief out of his sleeve. 'You've spilled some wine,' he murmured, leaning close and wiping the cloth slowly over her stomach. She saw a dark splash across her white skirt.

'Oh hell!' she hissed, grabbing the cloth off him and rubbing furiously, only making it worse. 'It won't come off! And this dress isn't even mine! It will cost a fortune to clean! And as for replacing it –'

'It looks like blood,' he remarked calmly, lifting the hem of her dress towards his nostrils. 'Smells like it, too.'

He let the dress drift back over her upper thighs. But then he dropped on to all fours like a hound and swayed over her.

'What will I do?' she mewed, dabbing the cloth on her legs. 'It will stain for ever!'

His hands flattened on either side of her sides, pinning her down on the cushions. 'I'll lick it off.'

For a moment his face hung white and suddenly fierce, inches away from hers. Fran was shivering, she realised, but not from fear. She was cold, surely that was all. The house hadn't been heated for centuries. Even the fire couldn't get a grip on the cold. The voice in her mind was getting weaker, but it squeaked from somewhere far away that she would have to fix that if she bought this house, along with the lighting.

Now he was blocking the fire completely. Her legs were stretched on either side of him. A log cracked loudly in the grate and she flinched. In that moment he darted forward and his mouth locked on to hers. His lips were firm and cold as they slid across hers, taking possession, holding her there. They seemed to be sucking something out of her, her breath, her life, everything was so still. Then his tongue slid, slim and slippery, into her mouth, and she jolted, her heart giving a kind of plunging leap back to life.

She pulled her face away, frowning at this stranger. 'You are mistaking me for another?'

His eyes were calm. 'Not at all. I know exactly who you are. I've been waiting for you.'

Fran gave a high, piping laugh to cover the intoxicating mix of discovery and recognition that was stirring forcefully inside her. She had wanted this house the moment she stepped inside. Now she wanted the owner.

'I don't understand you,' she whispered, shifting her legs under him and tweaking primly at her dress.

'No need to trouble yourself,' he answered, moving aside to let her sit up. 'You only need to know that you are mine now, and beyond redemption.' He cleared his throat. 'Also, your dress is ruined.'

Fran rubbed at the red patch. Already the stain felt dry and permanent.

'Well, perhaps you can tell me the secret of how you keep your own garments so pristine? Please find me some soap and water. If there is any water?'

He smiled, illustrating to perfection the phrase 'handsome devil'. 'I could, but you are not here to do laundry, are you?'

Fran leaned forward, aware of her breasts pushing out of her dress. 'I came to view your property.' She watched his hair lift under her breath and when she laughed he reached up, sensing her surrender, and pulled her down again on the cushions.

'There's wine on your neck,' he murmured, drawing his tongue across his teeth. 'Still looks just like blood.' One muscular thigh slid up under her dress, pushing her legs open. 'Still wish to see the rest of the house?'

'Later,' she breathed, as the life exhaled out of her. 'You can take me now.'

So he continued his task, rucking up the flimsy fabric of her dress until his velvety knee brushed against her fanny. Her cunt twitched violently at the contact, and at the draught brushing between their bodies. The costumier hadn't provided underwear. Should she not be wearing drawers, or knickerbockers? Because her bare pussy was pouting now against the pressure of his groin.

His eyes feasted on her large breasts spread beneath him, then he suddenly took the wineglass out of her hand and tipped the rest of the wine into her mouth. Some of it dribbled over her chin, and he licked it off. She swallowed and again felt the thick liquor flow through her veins, a dark potion rather than wine, seep into her head, spirals of intoxication.

'You are too untidy now to go to the ball.' He chuckled, letting a stream of wine thread through the cold air, drops splashing on her breasts, all over the doomed dress, soaking the cushions.

A squeal of protest wound up from her at the thought of the expense and hassle of getting this pure white muslin cleaned and purified.

He threw the glass aside, letting it shatter in the fireplace. 'You no longer look like a lady anyway, so I can do what I will.'

He pushed his mouth over her breasts, his breath cooling the skin, and Fran tangled her fingers in his silky hair, fine as water, and pushed his face into her cleavage. His teeth nipped and nibbled towards the aching nipples still trapped in the lace, and tore at the dress, sending a delicious rending of thin cotton into the silent air. Her breasts sprang free, swelling with desire as they met the air. She arched her back and he pushed her breasts together, the nipples rigid in the cold. His sharp teeth glinted briefly before clamping round one taut bud and biting it, hard.

She shrieked and opened her legs wider. She reached round to touch his buttocks, smooth and muscled beneath the buckskin breeches, then back to the front of his trousers where a row of mother-of-pearl buttons guarded his groin. Her fingers felt cold and claw-like as she rubbed them over the tightly fitting material, searching for some warmth emanating from the thick shape of his cock, but it was hard to get a grip. Her fingers kept slipping away.

He grabbed her wrists and pinned them over her head, his mouth still working on her nipples, and she brought her knees up round his hips, grinding her pussy against him. The dress was wrinkled round her waist and her bottom was cold on the floor as her legs tried to grip his bones, but all they found was air, as if they had no strength.

He was like a mirage, yet his mouth was so determined, sucking like a cub, taking in the point of the nipple and all the puckered skin around it. His sharp teeth drew ragged gasps from her and the cold air shrank her skin into needles of sensitivity. Her cunt was relaxing, waiting, wanting. She could hear the wet kiss of her pussy lips as she let him devour her.

Suddenly he lifted his head and sniffed the air like a dog. His eyes glittered over at the windows, then back at Fran, stretched out in the firelight.

'Don't dare stop now,' she hissed, her voice wild like an animal's.

He bared his teeth like a wolf, and his head snapped round again towards the window as if something had disturbed him. Delicious fear stirred in her belly, fuelled by ferocious excitement, and she arched herself at him again. As the flames filtered through her half-closed lashes she felt him slide away from her. Her breasts wobbled softly as he released them. She tried to drag him back but her fingers clawed at thin air and all she could see was the redness inside her eyelids.

* * *

Eric James cursed the traffic as he fitted the rusty key into the lock. He was twenty minutes late. The client had sounded dead classy on the phone. Not someone to keep waiting. And this house was proving the very devil to sell.

There was no sign of her. He groped for the light switches. Still no electricity. He marched into the ballroom and stopped. Someone was lying in front of the empty fireplace. Not just lying, but writhing and moaning. Shit. He didn't want to be responsible for some kind of accident in one of his high-end properties …

101

The figure moaned louder, and he saw that it was a woman arching her back, the sinews in her neck straining as she threw her head back and pushed her huge pale breasts invitingly into the moonlight falling in rectangles across the floor. Her legs were splayed wide, white flesh visible above white stockings, and her ripped dress was up round her waist.

He stepped closer. Something had evidently turned her on. Her buttocks bounced off the floor, her legs opening and closing, drawing his eye to her bush, but she wasn't fingering herself. In fact, her arms seemed pinned over her head.

Blood pumped into his balls. Eric glanced round the deserted house. Please God no one has double-booked this viewing …

'Miss Hughes?'

The girl swung her head from side to side, ringlets of hair unravelling around her ears. She lifted her legs and crossed them as if trying to trap something between them.

'Don't stop!' she groaned, offering up those glorious tits, those hard raspberry nipples. Her dress lay in tatters over her ribs and she had bitten her lip. There was blood on her chin. Her mouth and legs were open, wet, vacant, available, immediate possession, under offer, local search, all the office puns jostling in his head, and his cock grew stiff under the good tweed of his suit.

'Do it, just do it to me,' she urged, and Eric James didn't need telling twice.

* * *

So he was back. At last Fran could feel some real masculine weight on her, blocking out the cold air, and she gripped him with her legs once again. His shirt felt rougher than she remembered, and wasn't that the scrape of a zip rather than the sliding off of buttons?

Her eyes felt sticky, as if she'd been asleep for a hundred years. The man looming above her, edging his cock into her waiting cunt, had a square chin and broad shoulders, and instead of a white ruffled shirt he wore a jacket and tie. His hair was short. His mouth was closed. His eyes were blue.

It wasn't Frederick.

Fran screamed and struggled, but the newcomer shoved her down again.

'Where's Frederick?'

'Frederick?' The man shrugged. 'Nah. I'm the only one with keys.'

His fingers slid round to her pussy, burrowing into her, eyes watching her, while he opened her sex lips to expose her burning clit. His fingers were everywhere, strong, warm, insistent, up her arse, pushing into her cunt, and now his cock was pushing in. She didn't have the strength to stop him and ask where Frederick had gone.

Fran grabbed at his strong buttocks as his cock plunged right into her and they slithered like a single tentacled creature across the shiny floor. As he felt her fingers on him he reared back and slammed it back in, shoving them both with the force of it. Somehow she knew Frederick would have been gentler. But surely he would be back?

She crushed herself greedily against him in rhythm as he thrust in and out until she became fluid, sensations swirling and sharpening inside her as the wave approached. She wrapped her legs and arms round him like a cat, moaning as he strained himself backwards then kicked two mighty thrusts into her like knocking through a wall, and they both came in a violent explosion there in the moonlit ballroom.

There was silence for a long time, other than traffic passing in the street.

'Frederick was here,' Fran murmured, rolling away from him and staring at the corniced ceiling, which was webbed with cracks and runnels of damp. 'He was going to fuck me –'

'Oh, my God.' Eric sat up. 'Frederick Chalmers. The original owner of the house.' His blue eyes glowed at her, changing colour as she watched from blue to black. 'They said it was haunted. Which is why no one will buy it.'

Fran froze. 'I was nearly fucked by a ghost?'

Eric laughed. Cackled.

'Who could blame him, finding a damsel in a torn dress in his house?'

'He tore it. He gave me wine. He kissed me –' A taxi honked outside, and Fran jumped. The modern sounds elbowed out the sinister history licking around them. 'I should go!'

'Like that? You're practically naked!'

Eric fanned his hands out and touched her heavy breasts, squeezing them thoughtfully. Too late for any more viewings. The office would be closed now.

Fran's eyelids fluttered as excitement yawned and awakened inside her. She knelt up so he could reach her nipples, nibble and suck the way she liked it best. But, like Frederick, he started to bite, hard, until she yelped with pain, and then, as he pushed her back onto the floor to fuck her all over again, she caught that same wolfish grin she'd seen on Frederick, teeth glinting, lips red with blood, or wine, or just pleasure.

And then behind Eric's head she saw a figure cross in front of the fireplace. Spidery shadows jumped across the walls as the figure approached where she lay. It was him, back in charge of his own house, the white shirt open, the breeches tight, the grin splitting wider as he reached out hands like claws to pull Eric off her, holding him by the neck, squeezing the life out of him then tossing him aside like a rag.

And then he was fucking her, the sensations of his hands and mouth and cock heightened if anything, but how could she explain that it was like being fucked by water? Who indeed would she explain it to? Because now

105

Frederick was picking her up off the floor and together they floated away, up through the shadowy house.

The Ursa Legacy
Anne Tourney

Wrapped in the furs of my tribe, I sprawl beside the stone hearth and let the firelight lick my bare belly. The heat gilds my breasts, reddens my nipples. With my fingertips I trace the tattoo on my right breast, the sweeping signature of a bear's claw. The tattoo was my mate's gift to me when I joined his fierce, secretive clan. Now he lies between my legs, feasting. His furred jaws scrape my inner thighs, leaving ribbons of gooseflesh in their wake. I lift his head so I can read his eyes. His pupils are black with hunger.

Have we been lying here for days or hours? My smartphone, the palm-size tyrant that used to rule my life, stopped working the first time I entered the cave where the Ursines have feasted, fucked and celebrated for generations.

My mate's teeth nip the curves of my calves. His tongue

tickles the crevices below my knee, then glides up my leg to explore the furred cleft. I clutch handfuls of his coarse hair and push his mouth against my mound. As he bites at my ass, thighs and outer lips, I wonder how I ever tolerated the polite hesitancy of a human mouth. The creature I am now doesn't want to be licked to a delicate climax; she wants to be fucked into a roaring red abyss.

I pull my mate up to meet me, dragging him by the hair until we're lying face to face. I feel a deep growl building behind his ribs. I spread my legs and wait for him to enter me, but he rolls me over and pins me to the floor, his jaw gripping the nape of my neck. We rock back and forth, grunting. His paw covers my eyes and, in the darkness of his padded palm, I see the swirling crimson pool that signals a transformation. I bite down on his hand as I come. Accelerating his thrusts, he roars like a bear as we change together.

Each time we come like this, we transform each other, the way the first Ursines did when they began hunting, mating and breeding on Roaring Bear Peak. When I climax under his mouth, I'll become the beast I was meant to be.

One year ago this December, I never could have imagined what my life would become.

* * *

Less than ten shopping days remained before Christmas, and the skies were threatening snow. Those skies decided to release their load on the morning of our firm's first team-building retreat, which was to take place in the director's ski chalet on a 13,000-foot mountain peak known as Roaring Bear. As the van lurched up the snow-packed mountain pass, I suddenly sensed that we were being taken somewhere to be eaten. Here we were, all seven of the key personnel at Ursa Major Advertising, bundled into ski parkas and packed into an overheated van like stuffed quail in a chafing dish. As the vehicle rocked its way up the vertical road, I wondered if we'd survive the ride.

I glanced at Paul, the marketing director, and Tiffany, his lead graphic designer and not-so-secret sex slave. Both looked greenish-grey around the mouth, and Tiffany made soft retching sounds whenever the van bounced over a rut in the road. Behind the carsick couple sat Nick, a large, hulking man, hunched over a book. Lost in the pages, Nick didn't look remotely ill. I wasn't sure what Nick did at the firm, or why he'd been invited to this elite getaway. As far as I could tell, he worked in the mailroom. I only ever saw his towering form slipping soundlessly down to the basement, where I assumed he sorted mail with the other clerks. Next to Nick sat our executive designer Jayne, her creative partner Maude and our sales director Bob. I had a sudden vision of the entire executive team laid out nude on a banquet table, our mouths stuffed with baked apples, our greased skin glistening in the glow of a cosy fire.

But where was the hostess of this banquet? And where were we going, climbing the mountain to this snow-capped nowhere? When I looked out the window, all I could see were the black peaks of pine trees piercing a blanket of clouds. We were so far above the rest of the world that the lowest of those clouds engulfed the van in translucent fleece.

'Oh, Paul, I hope I'm not going to be sick,' Tiffany moaned. She leaned forward, her long golden hair draping her face. 'When will we get there?'

'I think we're getting close, darling.' Paul peered out the window. 'We're approaching a drive.'

Before Tiffany pranced into his life, I had been briefly and intensely intertwined with Paul for six months. Our workplace romance crash-landed when Tiffany joined Ursa Major. Although her skills as a graphic designer weren't anything spectacular, she had other assets that dazzled Paul.

I didn't want to think about Tiffany and Paul, or about the day I walked in on the two of them in Paul's office. Although I'd tried to obliterate the memory with dozens of Grey Goose martinis, I couldn't forget the sight of Tiffany splayed on Paul's desk, her pussy spread like a pink satin oyster as Paul feasted on her.

Paul had never intended to stop fucking me; he just wanted to add Tiffany to the mix and move me neatly to the side. But I had no intention of sharing a man with a woman who was younger, thinner and more servile than I'd ever be.

I forced my thoughts away from Tiffany's flawless nudity and focused on my new rabbit-fur boots, which fitted my calves as snugly as velvet gloves. The silk lining hugged my legs, and every time I shifted my feet I felt the sweet whisk of a rabbit's pelt against my skin. I knew it wasn't politically correct to wear genuine fur, but the thought of possessing the hide of a living being gave me a gut-level thrill.

'Love the boots, Melinda.'

A large male form filled the seat beside me. It was Nick, the mysterious mail clerk who'd somehow rated an invitation to this prestigious retreat. I'd never seen Nick up close. When we passed on the stairs, I saw nothing but a sheaf of black hair falling over his profile. He'd never even said hello to me; I only knew his name because I'd happened to see his badge one day. The sudden contact with his brown eyes startled me. He had a craggy face, but his full lips had a gently drawn curve that made me want to touch them. I flashed to an image of his mouth roving over my breasts. That flash of a fantasy, and what it revealed about the recent drought in my sex life, turned my neck and cheeks brick-red.

'We're almost there,' he said, covering my hand with his own. 'How are you doing?'

Nick's long fingers engulfed mine. I'm not a small woman, but I felt dwarfed by the mail clerk, who seemed to be in complete possession of the moment.

'I'm surviving, so far,' I said. 'I couldn't help but notice that you're the only passenger who doesn't look like he's about to puke.'

He smiled, the succulent mouth parting over strong teeth. 'I grew up around here,' he said.

'I didn't think anyone lived on Roaring Bear year round, besides mountain lions and squirrels. Where did you go to school?'

'My mother taught me at home. She's never been a big advocate of mainstream education.'

Nick squeezed my hand, ending the brief conversation. When the vehicle stopped, there was an outburst of relieved laughter and applause, followed by shocked silence as we gazed up at the structure that towered over us. Not a chalet, more like a medieval fortress, the building rose against the foot of the mountain like an outcropping of the mountain itself. Only the illuminated first-storey windows made the structure look remotely inviting. A double row of fir trees encircled the chalet like dark sentinels.

'We're here, Melinda,' Nick said softly into my ear, as if we were the only two whose arrival mattered.

He took my hand to help me down from the van, then wrapped me in his arms and lifted me down the last two steps. His body was hard, packed with muscle, and warm as a furnace under his woollen overcoat. I thought I could feel his heart thrumming through the cloth. Though I'm not exactly a lightweight, my body cleared the ground, and for a second I was airborne in his arms.

When my feet in their rabbit-skin boots touched the ground, my toes tingled, as if they had made contact with a long-lost home.

* * *

'There are two types of living things on this planet,' said the fifty-something brunette with the staggering cleavage.

Regina stood addressing her executive staff. The firelight framed her regal curves as she tantalised us with a long pause. I glanced around the ancient oak table, which looked like the battered door of a drawbridge. Paul and Tiffany held hands. Their faces were frozen in rapt attention. As our boss, Regina already had a hold on our daily lives. As our hostess tonight, she had her velvet grip on our souls as well.

'There are predators, and prey,' Regina continued. 'As humans, we're the only species that has the luxury of deciding which group we'll join.'

'Which one are you?' Nick whispered in my ear.

Nick occupied the chair next to mine, his mass warming my body as his arm swept around the back of my chair. I gasped when his lips whisked my earlobe. Regina glanced over at us and I froze. The woman had been my boss for three years, but I still stammered and blushed whenever she towered over my desk at Ursa Major.

On the table around us lay the remains of our meal, a rich, flesh-heavy feast. We had sampled fowl, pork, beef and fish, with no trace of greenery or roughage in sight. After the drive up the mountain, we were all famished. Even Tiffany gorged on roast duck, and her full lips still glistened from the grease. We all sipped a full-bodied cabernet as we listened to Regina speak. Lapped by the golden tongues of the fire, she was a beast-goddess aflame.

Nick's hand clutched the edge of my chair. His fingers remained at a discreet distance from my thigh, but I could sense their heat. I had felt him watching me as I ate, his eyes travelling back and forth from my lips to the meat piled on my fork. Meat had never tasted so good to me; the rich flavour of pork, beef and duck filled my belly and warmed my blood. Their juices lingered on my tongue.

'Let's get out of here,' he said. He tugged at the sleeve of my sweater. 'I want to show you something.'

'Are you kidding?' I hissed. 'Regina will kill us.'

'She won't mind. Trust me.'

114

He was right. As he pulled my chair back, her dark eyes settled on us briefly, and I thought her mouth curved into a smile. Paul and Tiffany glared at us as if they were personally offended by our departure. Nick's hand rested in the small of my back as he guided me out of the dining room and into the large kitchen. The stone floor was littered with feathers and spotted with blood, the cryptic signs of a fresh kill. A burly woman with thick arms was wiggling the wing of a large bird, trying to yank it from its socket. When she saw Nick, her broad face split into a grin.

'If it ain't the young master,' she said, holding out her arms. 'Almost too big for your old Peg, aren't you?' As the big woman engulfed Nick in her embrace, the pieces of this strange story fell together.

'You grew up here, didn't you?' I said, as Nick broke away from the cook and led me out of the kitchen. We walked through a warren of hallways lined with stone like the interior of a mediaeval castle. I stopped, hands on hips. 'You're Regina's son.'

Nick grinned. 'You catch on fast.'

'But you're a mail clerk!'

His grin turned into a rich, coarse laugh, like an animal's growl. 'I'm not a mail clerk, Melinda. I'm an account executive, like you. I work in the basement because I'm comfortable in that part of the building. It's dark and private – my own secret den.'

'I'm such an idiot.'

'Hardly. You're by far the smartest executive at the agency. That's why we chose you. One of the reasons, anyway.' He looked me over with a combination of lust and hunger that made me feel like a trapped animal, a quivering bunny in my rabbit-fur boots.

'Chose me for what?'

'Don't ask yet.'

'Why? What am I supposed to –'

Nick silenced me with his lips. As his hard arms enveloped me, all resistance seeped from my muscles and I went slack in his arms. His tongue parted my lips and his knee slipped between my thighs. My feet rose from the ground as desire rose in my belly; I felt as if I were being lifted by my longing. Since my ugly rupture with Paul, I'd been in a sexual slumber. I'd never imagined that the shy, overgrown kid who looked like a mail clerk would be the one to wake me from my prolonged nap.

Nick's hands were warm as they met the soft skin under my sweater. When he touched my belly, I felt his hardness against my pubic mound, and, if he'd ripped off my tights at that moment, I'd have let him take me in the hallway.

But he stopped.

'Not here,' he whispered. 'I need to show you something.' He pulled me down the hallway to a large, heavy door, which he opened. A full moon illuminated the snow, and the clear black sky was studded with a glittering extravagance of stars. The night was glorious, but the cold sliced my exposed cheeks like a steel blade.

'We're going out there?' I whined. 'I don't even have my coat!'

'Here. Take mine.'

Nick took the overcoat that he'd been wearing on our drive to the chalet and wrapped me in its depths. The heavy wool held his scent, a rich smell that blended musk and sweat with the clean astringency of pine needles. The cloth was so warm that it might as well have been resting on a wood-burning stove. As I buttoned the coat around my body, Nick knelt before me in the snow. A crown of snowflakes twinkled in his hair. In the silver light, with his moon shadow spilling around his knees like a cloak, he reminded me of an ancient king.

'Are you proposing?' I joked.

He grinned. 'Not yet. For now I just want you to climb on my back.'

'You can't be serious. Nick, I'm no Barbie doll.'

'I'm aware of that. That's another reason why you're perfect. Get on.'

It occurred to me that Regina might have arranged this scenario, that she might even be recording us somehow on a hidden video camera. Maybe this was one of those trust-building exercises that account executives had to endure at company retreats. I had to be able to trust

Nick to bear my weight. If I couldn't relinquish my Type A lust for control, I'd be picked apart by the rest of the management team at Ursa Major. Of course, I'd be even more humiliated if Nick's back buckled as he tried to lift me.

'Listen, Melinda,' Nick said, breaking into my thoughts, 'the snowdrifts out there are as high as your waist. There's no way you can walk to the place where we're going.'

'And where is that?'

My paranoid fantasy of the trust-building exercise was replaced by an image of myself being ripped apart and eaten by Nick out in a snowy meadow under the full moon. Oddly enough, the vision didn't bother me. In fact, the thought of his hands staking their claim on my body, his hardness penetrating me on this frosty night, flooded my pussy with a tingling heat.

'Do you really think I'm going to tell you?' he said with a laugh.

Before I could respond, he lunged forward so that his body was wedged between my legs. As if I weighed nothing at all, he spun me with his hands so that I faced forward. With me riding on top of him, he loped into the snow. The crusted white surface gave way like powder in front of him, his thick thighs tossing clouds of glittering silver dust into the air. He ran up and down the wooded slopes in long, canted strides, navigating the pines and bare aspens as if he knew each tree individually. I gripped his neck, ducking to avoid the low branches of the trees, my mouth nuzzling his thick, damp hair. His skin steamed from the exertion, and, as I clung to him, my body shook to the rhythm of his panting breath.

Even though I wasn't the one running up a mountain with a full-grown woman on my back, the thin air at this altitude had left me short of breath. Regina's chalet was nestled at a dizzying 10,000 feet, but we had ascended past the tree line. Now Nick was climbing a rugged trail studded with boulders. His big hands used the rocks to bear our weight while his feet struggled for purchase on the slope. When we finally crested the trail, we were both fighting for breath.

We had reached the mouth of a cave, which was sealed by a large wooden door. Nick knelt in the snow, and I climbed off his back, my legs trembling. We stood for a moment under the dazzling mantle of stars, with acres of stone and shadowed woodland stretching out below us. The moon glowed in an eerie inversion of night, turning the landscape into the negative of a black-and-white photograph.

I glanced at Nick. He was watching me, his eyes dark in the moonlight.

'You brought me here for a reason, didn't you?' I asked.

'For several reasons, actually.'

'Where are we? What is this place?'

'One of my favourite places in the world. You might say it's a childhood hideout.'

He pushed open the wooden door of the cave. The darkness that engulfed us had a mammalian smell, like the fur and milk of an animal that's just given birth. Nick struck a match and lit candles that hung in sconces on the walls. The cavern yawned, extending so deep into the mountain that it vanished into blackness.

'Some hideout,' I remarked.

Except for a large bearskin rug, the room was unfurnished. Tapestries hung on the walls, their rich colours almost untouched by time. In red, gold and brown thread were the images of dozens of beasts. I stepped closer. Most of the animals on these storybook tapestries were bears, or human–bear hybrids: hunting, mating, merging. They tore at each other with teeth and claws, feasted on each other's flesh. As I studied the pictures, I felt Nick's heat surround me.

'What is this?' I whispered.

'The story of my tribe.'

'What tribe?'

'We call ourselves the Ursines now, but for centuries our name couldn't be translated into anything you'd understand.'

'Ursines,' I repeated. 'As in bears.'

My voice had its usual sceptical edge, but standing in this feral den, with Nick's broad torso pressed to me and his thick arms encircling me, his fingers rough against my skin, I felt anything but sceptical. I thought of Regina standing at the head of the table, the silver amulet she always wore glowing at the crest of her breasts. I'd never thought about that abstract shape, and the pendant had become so familiar to me that I hardly noticed it any more. Now I recalled the form of a bear's claw wrought in sterling silver.

'That's right.'

'So you and your mother and presumably everyone in your family are not human.'

'No. Not entirely. Although we clean up nicely for the right people.'

'Do you eat humans?' My eyes fell on the illustration of a human female, nude, her thighs spread to receive a male bear hybrid.

'Sometimes. But, for us, eating humans is more of a rite of passage than anything else. It's something that we do when we bring a new female into the tribe. Regina was the last new female. As her son, I'm now looking for our next mate.'

'I suppose you think that's me,' I said.

'I know it's you, Melinda. I've known for over a year. I've watched you walking, eating, laughing, fighting with the other execs. You're passionate and strong. And you just happen to be gorgeous.'

'And to think I assumed you spent the day sorting mail,' I joked weakly.

I couldn't see Nick's face, but I could feel his body

transforming. A change coursed through him like the urgency that comes before the first pulsating spasms of a climax.

'No. I spent my days wanting you. And I've spent night after night thinking about you, dreaming about bringing you here and taking you.'

'I think I should have a say in this, Nick. Especially in the part about being taken. Taken where?'

'Where do you think?' His teeth sank into the nape of my neck, and I almost collapsed.

'I don't know what to think. I don't even know if this is real.'

'Melinda, it's real. I know it's hard to believe, but, if you want the Ursa legacy, it's yours. All you have to do is say yes.'

'What's in it for me?'

'Everything.' Nick laughed. 'You'll own Roaring Bear Peak, and you'll be the queen of our tribe after Regina steps down. You'll have everything you had in your human life, and so much more. You'll be one of us. One of them.'

He pointed to the ursine creatures that cavorted and feasted and fucked on the tapestries. Draped in the glorious reds and blues of pure carnage, they celebrated their freedom, their animal greed. What did I have in my life right now that could compare to that carnal glory? I owned a condo the size of an icebox, with mortgage payments so high that I could barely pay for my dry cleaning. My sex life had turned into a desert, and forget about love or longing. I couldn't remember the last time I'd been stirred by a desire for anything I couldn't charge to a credit card.

'Do you want this?' Nick asked.

His teeth nicked my earlobe as he spoke into my ear. With his chest pressed against my back, the rhythm of his heart shook my ribcage. My own heart picked up his accelerated beat, synchronising our pulses. A low roar, like the groan of a faraway sea, filled my head. At first I thought the roar came from the cave itself, from the spirits of the bears and half-bears represented in the livid hues of these tapestries. Then I realised that the sound came from deep inside my own gut.

'I want it.'

I spun around and clutched Nick's crotch, just in case he missed my not-so-subtle request. His hard length more than filled my hand. Nick smiled as he pulled off the heavy woollen coat and peeled off my turtleneck sweater.

'Want what?' he teased.

'All of it. Give it to me.'

In the dark cavern of my own body, a new spirit was taking shape. She held all of the hunger and anger and power that I'd kept securely locked down since I left the feral realm of childhood. She embodied the monsters of my earliest dreams and the she-bears that ravaged my fairytale fantasies. Nick's mouth was slick against mine, his breath drawing that rising spirit to the surface. When he bent to bite my breasts, I hardly felt the sharp edges of his teeth. I'd grown a new skin, tougher than any human's. My new hide was covered with a velvet pelt, the same cinnamon-brown as my hair.

For a second I thought I must have fallen into a lavish, surreal dream. Then I saw Nick's face, and I knew that the pelt was no trick of the subconscious. His brown eyes glittered with a beast's uncontrolled appetites as he pulled me down onto the floor. His hands were human, but black claws tipped his fingers, and, when I held up my own hands to grab his shoulders, I saw that I had the same claws. His sable fur covered his chest and shoulders, tapering into a peak at his sternum. The dark line burst into a thick brush of hair at his groin. His cock rose from the brush, red as lifeblood.

'Tell me,' Nick ordered. His voice had thickened into a growl. 'Can you take it?'

I lay back and took in the sight of his torso, the magnificent thighs, the parabola of his erection. The ghosts of the ancient Ursines surged around Nick, covering him in veils of red and orange. One moment, he was pure bear; the next, he was a glorious man. And when I said yes, and he lowered himself into me, we merged as members of the same tribe. The climax built so slowly that it was almost painful, and, when the pleasure erupted inside me, I knew I had left the fragile trappings of my old self behind. The roar that burst from my mouth when I came sounded nothing like my own voice.

* * *

We mated, parted, dozed, woke and mated again throughout the night. In the interludes between our ravenous fucks, Nick told me about the Ursines. The tribe's recorded history began before the tapestries; there were caves in Europe and Asia where stories of the ancient Ursines were etched in stone. Regina, as the primary Ursa and heiress to this tribe's matriarchal legacy, had the authority to bring human women into the tribe. She also had the power to transform at will, not simply when she was overtaken by animal appetites. Her son's mate would inherit that power, along with miles of wooded mountain, the chalet, a penthouse in the city and a cavern filled with the gleaming treasures seized from human beings through the ages.

And, when Regina stepped down, I would become the Executive Director of Ursa Major. But, if this corporate retreat was turning into a fairytale, who had chosen me to play the princess?

'My mother has had her eye on you for months,' Nick said.

I stroked the whorls of fur that lined his limbs and belly, which were neither animal nor human.

'Was all this arranged for me?' I asked.

'Not entirely. My mother cares deeply about the agency. It's her connection to the human world. She wields her human power at Ursa Major, and her ursine power here on the mountain.'

'Speaking of Ursa Major, shouldn't we be getting back to the retreat?'

Nick grinned and pulled me on top of him. I gasped when his cock filled me.

'One more time,' he said. 'I want to hear you roar again.'

* * *

A blizzard was taking shape over the mountain when we finally returned to Regina's chalet, and sheets of snow spun from a leaden sky. Even before we reached the chalet, we heard the commotion – raised voices, barking dogs. A crowd had gathered in front of the chalet and, from the urgency in their voices, I knew this wasn't a team-building exercise. Dressed in heavy coats and bearing loaded backpacks, the crowd looked more like a search-and-rescue team.

'Nick. You're back, thank God.'

The tall form of a statuesque woman separated itself from the crowd. Regina strode up to us. Like the others, she was dressed for a mountaineering expedition. The tension in her face melted briefly as she saw me. Her sharply etched nostrils twitched, as if she could smell the evidence of last night's mating. After quickly looking me over, she took me into her arms and hugged me. Her hug held me like a steel trap.

'Welcome,' she whispered.

'What happened?' Nick asked. 'What's going on?'

Regina released me, but her hand clung to mine. 'Paul and Tiffany are missing. They left early with the others this morning to ski before breakfast. The ski party lost track of them in the woods, and they still haven't been found. Nick, can you help? The others are exhausted. They've been searching for hours. You know the woods better than anyone.'

Nick and his mother stared at each other for a long moment. Then Regina's blood-brown eyes turned to me. I tried to stand up to her stare, but I wasn't strong enough. Not yet.

'I think I know where we can find them,' Nick said.

Before I could speak to Regina, Nick pulled me onto his back again, and we were off. Our trek was a repetition of last night, only without the magic of starlight. As we sped past the trees that were now becoming familiar to me, I wondered how I could return to my life in the city now that my human skin had been stripped away.

The snow fell in opaque blankets, a whiteout that left no room to see the woods, much less the narrow path. If

I'd had the strength to whine, I would have asked Nick why he hadn't left me back at the chalet with the woman who was going to share her realm with me. My hands were frozen solid to Nick's neck, and my belly was an empty cauldron of hunger. I could be back at the chalet now, enjoying a plate of rare meat and a mug of mulled wine, instead of wandering through the snow searching for a man I loathed and his silly fuck-toy.

But I suddenly realised that I didn't loathe Paul any more. For the first time in months, I could think of Paul and Tiffany without being swept over by a tsunami of resentment. All those feelings – the rage, the jealousy, the burned-out desire for Paul – seemed like emotions in miniature. My new appetites and sensations were vast, overpowering.

Nick lurched to a halt in the thigh-deep powder. I had to choke him to keep from flying over his shoulders. In the shroud of snow, I couldn't see him, but I could feel the tremor that coursed through his body as he sniffed the air.

'They're here,' he said. 'In the ranger's shed.'

'How do you know?'

'I smell them. Don't you? Smell the air, Melinda. Learn to use your new gifts.'

'All I smell is snow,' I grumbled. I sniffed, then sniffed again, until I finally caught the fragrance of live flesh. It smelled nothing like the artificial odours that mask the civilised human body: soap, toothpaste, perfume. This scent was thoroughly alive, like the warm, bloody reek of a newborn lamb.

My stomach clenched with a response that would have sickened me yesterday. The old Melinda didn't get hungry at the scent of humans. But then, the old Melinda was human, too.

Through the snow, I watched Nick shovel the snow away from the door of the ranger's shed with his hands. He had to shove the door open with his shoulder, throwing his entire weight against the wood. I heard the door give way under his weight with a crack and a groan; I heard the weak, grateful cries of the humans inside.

I waded through the powder to join my mate at the door of the shed. Paul and Tiffany clung to each other on the floor like Hansel and Gretel in the woods. Compared to Nick, Paul seemed as fragile and as frivolous as a ceramic doll. Tiffany's throat was bright red from the cold. The blood coursing through her carotid artery sent a tremor through her smooth skin. I had seen Tiffany nude on that day I caught her with Paul, and I could still visualise the twin curves of her breasts, tipped with pink gumdrop nipples. I pictured the firm heart that throbbed under her ribs, the tender young liver and the juicy innards nestled under that taut abdomen, and my belly rumbled.

Paul smiled at me with the gratitude of a man about to be rescued. His lips were cracked and pale, but I remembered when that mouth would rise from between my thighs, slick with my juices.

Nick took my hand and squeezed. 'It's a rite of passage,' he reminded me in a whisper. 'This is how you claim the legacy.'

A long moment passed, in which the four of us hung suspended in the mystery that lay ahead, then Nick and I fell on our prey. The ranger's hut turned into a red chamber of screams and open flesh and flying claws. Behind a veil of flying blood and falling snow, atop a mountain that would be mine, my new life began.

Finally the humans were silent, and my mate and I feasted.

Riding the Ghost Train
Chrissie Bentley

I awoke with a start. Was that laughter I heard? It took me a moment to remember where I was, to connect the hard metallic ridges beneath me with the barely carpeted floor in the back of Ryan's van, and the absolute stygian darkness with the fact that we were parked in a clearing in the middle of the park. Ryan lay on his side beside me, his slow, rhythmic breathing letting me know that whatever I'd heard had not awakened him, although the thick weight that pressed against my thigh told me that not all of his faculties were sleeping.

I shifted myself slightly, to mould my buttocks around the bulge – we were both fully clothed, but the night had grown chilly enough that we'd happily draped the comforter over us as we sat talking, listening, waiting. Then, though neither of us had any intention of doing so, we must have fallen asleep.

Sleep was out of the question now, though. Yes, that was laughter. And, faint behind it, voices, cheery and excited. Snatches of music, too, and, underpinning them, the low hum of machinery. I wondered what I'd see if I sat up and wiped the condensation off the back windows. The pitch-black of Whiskeyport Springs Park, one summer night in 2011? Or a scene from one of the sepia photographs that hung in frames around Ryan's office wall, preserving this place as it was a century ago?

I closed my eyes and nestled closer to Ryan; he stirred slightly and an arm looped around me, the side of his wrist just grazing my breast. I wriggled to try to make firmer contact – we weren't dating, we weren't lovers, we hadn't even kissed. But if I'd ever needed to feel another human being close alongside me, now was that moment.

I'd met Ryan a week ago ... a little under a week ago. The mercury had been in the high 90s and my house was stifling, even with the A/C cranked up full. Outside, though, there was enough of a breeze to make the heatwave seem bearable, so I grabbed a paperback and some breadcrumbs for the swans and took myself off to the park for the day.

Things had changed since I was there last ... Isn't it strange how, when you live on top of some place, you hardly ever go there? The park was five minutes' walk from my house, but it must have been five years since I'd last been down there. They'd landscaped the river banks, planted new trees and, up over the rise where the picnic benches sit, the local archaeological society had hung a sign welcoming visitors to the Whiskeyport Funland excavation. A handful of volunteers stood around, so I wandered over towards them. 'I didn't know this place was even here.'

'Most people don't.'

He was tall, dirty-blond fading to bald, early forties probably. Good-looking. Wore his clothes well. A nametag pinned to his shirt insisted I call him Ryan.

'Can I just wander about in there?' I asked.

Ryan looked around. 'If you like. We haven't got all the signs up yet, though, so, if you don't mind waiting a moment, in case anyone else wants a tour, I'd be happy to give you the full treatment.'

'OK.'

Ten minutes later, the pair of us were standing beside a grassy mound on which a large rectangle was marked out with tiny orange flags and wire. Gorse bushes pocked the perimeter and a medium-sized horse-chestnut tree sent its roots cascading through the middle. 'This is where the Hall of Mirrors used to stand. It burned down in 1927 and, when the park closed at the end of that season, that was it, they never reopened.'

'You can't really blame them,' I murmured. 'They did have a lot of bad luck.'

According to Ryan's practised narration, the Hall of

Mirrors was only the last of half a dozen rides to have burned, collapsed or simply stopped working in five years.

'It was the nature of the beast. A lot of the old amusement parks were in serious financial trouble by the late 1920s – their golden age was before the First World War; after that, they were treading water at best. So they cut back on staff, cut down on repair work, and safety went out of the window. It's as likely that someone torched the place for the insurance money as that it was an accident.' He paused and led the way through a dense thicket, to where a few stubs of metal still protruded from the soil. 'This was the last ride they opened, a ferris wheel, in 1923.'

I nodded, surprised to find myself so fascinated by all this, and murmured once again, 'It's amazing. I had no idea that this place even existed.'

'We've been excavating here for a couple of years,' Ryan explained. 'Nothing serious – we're not talking about the Valley of the Kings, after all. But it's amazing how many little things you find if you go an inch or so below the topsoil. Tokens for the rides, pieces of the rides. Most of the wood and materials were taken away by the locals after the park closed; you find them in local antique stores every so often, old metal signs, mainly, but better things as well. Come this way.' He reached out and took my arm; a little surprised, I let him.

'This was the centre of the park, a huge carousel. You can still see the central hub. We actually found one of the horses just over there. It was broken, of course, but it's being restored. We're planning to open a small museum here.'

'It's kind of a sad place, isn't it?' I mused. 'It must have been so grand once, and now it's just a wilderness.'

Ryan smiled. 'I like to come here at night, just sit in the dark and imagine what it must have been like back then. Sometimes ...' His voice trailed away.

'Sometimes?' I asked.

'Nothing. I was going to say, sometimes you can hear things. I've spent the night here a few times, settled down in the back of my van, and just let my imagination go.'

I smiled. 'What sort of things?'

He looked at me curiously. 'People, music, machinery ... like I said, I like to let my imagination go. But you're right, it is sad.'

We walked on. Every few minutes, he'd pause to point out another lost landmark; every so often, too, I got the distinct impression that he wanted to say something else, only to change his mind at the last moment. I looked at him and wondered what he did when he wasn't grubbing around in the remains of an old amusement park. Instead, I asked him about the proposed museum.

'If you really want to see what we've found –' he rummaged in his jacket pocket and pulled out a business card '– I'm there most weekdays. We have a few small displays set up, and more stuff in the back room.'

I took the card. 'Thanks. I'll come down maybe one afternoon this week. I'm Chrissie, by the way.'

He nodded enthusiastically. 'Great. I'll look forward to it.'

True to my word, I dropped by the following Friday afternoon. Ryan's face visibly brightened as I walked in, and I couldn't help but notice how cute, boyish, it made him look. I really hadn't paid that sort of attention before; to my own still lingering surprise, I really was more interested in the old park. I'd often considered becoming 'involved' in local community activities, but had never come across any that appealed. This – the Friends of Funland Restoration Project – was different.

I delved into my purse and pulled out a book, *Whiskeyport Funland in Old Postcards*. 'I picked this up on Monday. The place was beautiful.'

Ryan smiled. 'If I'd known you were that keen, I could have given you a copy – we've got hundreds in the basement. It wasn't exactly a best-seller.'

'Never mind.' It didn't seem appropriate to tell him I'd found it in the remainders store for $1.98.

We spent the afternoon talking and touring the museum, such as it was, and, when he asked if we could meet up again later, I just laughed and suggested we make it much later. His stories of the things he'd heard, or thought he'd heard, on the nights he spent in Funland intrigued me. 'Why don't we go there together? Tonight?'

He looked at me curiously. 'Really?'

'Really. I haven't spent a night in a haunted house since I was a schoolgirl. Maybe I'll tell you about it tonight. And I'll bring the marshmallows.'

Home again, I dressed for a night in the back of a van – a T-shirt with a sweater thrown over my shoulder, jeans, sneakers – and was pleased to find Ryan looking just as casual; it meant he wasn't thinking of this as any kind of date. In fact, he was so practical that, if I had had any romantic thoughts in mind, a look inside his backpack would have chased them right off: a couple of meaty paperbacks, a reading light, a bag of tacos and some bottled water. 'Now, remember, I never promised we'd see or hear anything,' he said, as we settled down for the night. 'But if you lie back quietly, and let your mind wander …'

Something was certainly wandering now. The hand that I'd been gently trying to manoeuvre had slipped to cup my entire left breast; I could feel my nipple pressing into his palm, and a gentle answering pressure coming back at me. His breathing had changed imperceptibly as well. I think it was safe to say he was awake.

I lay still. The voices had faded outside, although I could still hear the music, too faint for me to actually make out a melody, but definitely there all the same. I wondered what time it was – some nights, if the wind was in the right direction, I could hear the Pontiac Grill letting people out around 1.30 or 2 a.m., despite the fact that it was a good couple of miles from my house. From here, it was barely a mile away. Give it a strong breeze to ride on, and no wonder it seemed so loud.

Ryan's fingers tightened softly around my breast, and the bulge pressing into my ass flexed too, straining against the layers of denim that lay between us. I wondered how I should react; whether I should maintain the pretence of sleeping. It sounds daft, but sometimes it's nice just to lie there being cuddled, and I knew – or thought I knew – that Ryan was too much of a gentleman to try forcing the issue.

At the same time, though, there was another gentle thrust against my buttock and, as his arm drew me closer to him, I felt his breath warm against the back of my neck for the first time. OK, that feels good. I drew my own arm up tighter against my body, trapping his one hand against my breast, while I let my free arm rest on my side, the tip of my pinkie just grazing the weave of his jeans. He kissed the nape of my neck softly, and I shifted my hand a little, to rest on his hip.

This was fun. He'd make a move; I'd make one back at him. He squeezed my breast; I pushed my hand between our bodies – not so far that I would break the contact, nor even so far that I could touch his cock through the cloth, but close enough that he knew I might, and close enough that I knew I wanted to. We still hadn't spoken.

His hand was on my belly now, his fingers gently kneading my skin through my T-shirt, at the same time as he slowly ... very slowly ... dragged the fabric up. I suddenly realised that I was holding my breath, anticipating the first thrill of his fingertips on my bare skin. For the first time since we met, I wondered what sort of lover he would turn out to be. He'd certainly been gentle and patient up until now – even if he was asleep when that erection first came on, still it had done nothing more than tantalise me so far, and my hand slipped a little further down, my own fingertips aching to sketch its shape in my mind.

He understood my movement and, as his hand slipped onto my waistband, he shifted his hips slightly, away from my body. I didn't move. The moment was so perfect, the two of us poised on the edge of discovery, well aware of the ease with which we could take that one final step, but holding ourselves back, savouring those spine-tingling seconds that too few lovers ever take the time to enjoy.

He kissed me again, on the side of my neck, and I thought of turning my head to meet his lips. Then the night exploded into noise, the clatter of machinery grinding into motion, reverberating through the interior of the van and shattering whatever last pretence of sleeping either of us was entertaining.

It could not have lasted more than a second or two; before I'd even sat up and caught my breath, all was silent again. Beside me, Ryan was breathing heavily, and the hand that now lay on mine was shaking slightly. Or was that me? 'What was that?' I whispered.

'I don't know. I've never heard anything like that before.'

The noise boomed again, but this time it did not fade away completely; instead, it just receded into the distance somewhat, then started coming around again. Like a small locomotive on a short loop of track.

'Where did you say we were parked?' I asked, although I clearly remembered what he'd said as we parked. We were in the middle of the old Ghost Train.

Ryan was on his knees, looking out of the back window. 'There's nothing out there,' he muttered, but I still jumped when the van creaked as he crawled back alongside me. 'What do you want to do?'

'I don't know,' I answered slowly. 'I mean, we came out here to listen to the ghosts. It'd be stupid to turn and run now, wouldn't it?'

I told him what I'd heard before he woke up; how I convinced myself the sounds were simply coming in on the wind. I glanced down at my watch – it was later than I thought, gone three o'clock already. Obviously, I'd convinced myself wrongly.

My heart was beating at a manageable rate again, and I lay back down. Our hands were still twined together.

'Sure you're OK?' he asked.

'Yeah. It just gave me a start. I wonder what it was.'

He was silent. I knew what he was thinking, but he didn't say it. Instead: 'It certainly broke the moment, didn't it?'

I laid my hand on his shoulder. 'It did, rather. I hate to think what would have happened if it had started a few minutes later.'

He laughed. 'With luck, we wouldn't even have noticed.' Raising himself, he kissed me on the lips, then broke away again. 'Listen. Are those the voices you heard?'

All around the van, the hum of happy chatter had resumed. Occasionally, one voice – a child's here, a man's there – broke through the buzz, but not so far that you could make out the words.

I clasped Ryan to me. 'Do you think … if we can hear them, do you think they can see us?'

'I don't know. If they can, they probably think we're part of one of the machines. And don't forget where we're parked. If we are inside the Ghost Train, we're probably in darkness, anyway.'

A memory came back to me: the first time I went to a funfair with a boy. I was still a kid … still at school, anyway … and had never done anything more than kiss and hold hands. And that's all we did this time, until we got onto the Ghost Train and, without a word of warning, he pressed my hand into his lap. My shriek was even louder than the banshees howling around us, and, when the ride ended, he ran like the wind. Well, what goes around comes around and, all these years later, here I am back on the same old ride. The only difference is, I'm not afraid of boys' laps any more. But am I afraid of ghosts?

I could still hear the voices. Before, when they came, it was in bursts, a few minutes of noise that then faded away. Not this time. There was a new constancy to them, as though whatever barrier they'd been pushing through earlier had finally given way. The awful roaring noise had not returned, but the music was back, and a distant popping sound – a rifle range, maybe? I could smell popcorn.

Ryan was silent, his arms locked around me, his breathing shallow. I pressed my body against his; the bulge in his pants had subsided, and I felt a peculiar disappointment. Does fear make people horny? I don't know – I'm not even sure if I was horny. But, though it sounds clichéd, feeling his hardness pushing against me conveyed a sense of reality that balanced the sheer unreality of what I was hearing outside. Without even thinking about what I was doing, I pressed my hips harder against his loins, and started to gently gyrate.

He moaned slightly and I increased the pace a little, triumphant as I felt the first stirrings answer my movements. We didn't speak, we didn't kiss. This wasn't lust talking, or passion. If you want to be horribly analytical about it, it was two people surrounded by something they didn't understand, seeking comfort in the one thing they knew they could rely on. Or, at least, that's my story, and I'm sticking to it.

I pushed and rolled him onto his back, then plunged my face into his neck, biting and sucking at the flesh, the night's growth of beard stabbing tiny exciting needles into my lips and cheek. My hands tugged at his T-shirt, pulling it out of his pants (why do so many men insist on tucking in their Ts?) and hoisting it over his chest. I located a nipple and swirled my tongue around it. For all his blondness, he was surprisingly hairy; I let my fingers run through the curls while I sought out his other nipple and, opening my mouth as wide as I could, sucked his flesh into my mouth.

I felt his hands tugging at my jeans, fumbling with the button. I moved away slightly. 'Not yet,' I whispered. In truth, I didn't want to be naked there and then – was it my imagination, or had the voices outside increased in volume? I wondered what time sunrise was. It couldn't be long now. But would it even make a difference?

His hands fell away; I hoped he wasn't disappointed. I thought of saying something reassuring, but didn't. Actions speak louder than words – I bit into his stomach. He groaned loudly, so I did it again. That's it, make a noise. That's what I want to hear. When he cried out, I couldn't hear the sounds outside. I bit down again, but now I was unbuckling his belt, and popping open the clip of his jeans. I pulled at the waistband; he raised his hips, and his jeans and boxers slipped down, and the musky scent of his cock rose to meet me, free at last.

I felt my pussy flood; I'd forgotten how long it had been since I last … I held him in one hand, measuring him in my mind. Longer than I'd guessed, and thinner, too, but thin in a good way; thin enough that I could really work my lips and tongue on him, rather than straining wide to simply envelop him. Men forget, or perhaps they never knew, mouths don't stretch like pussies, a girl needs a little leeway, something to get a firm grip on.

I buried my face into his balls, feeling his shaft hard against my cheek. I licked coarsely at the hairy skin, sucking slightly, then breaking away to bite into his inner thigh. He gasped – in pain? In surprise? I didn't care. Now I took one whole ball into my mouth, swirling it against my teeth and cheeks, then released it as I licked up his shaft.

His cock was my whole world now; the sounds from outside a less than irrelevant backdrop to his breathing and moans. I moistened the head of his prick with my tongue, then dragged it over my cheeks and lips. He spoke. 'Please, suck me.' I responded with a little nip, taking the very tip of his dick between my teeth and biting down. Not hard this time, just enough for him to feel the pressure, and for me to feel that wonderful silky firmness. His breath drew in sharply; I took him deeper, feeling my lips slip over his helmet, and then closing my mouth around his shaft and holding him there, drawing out his flavour with slow, luxurious sucks.

My hands were on his thighs, my nails pulling at the flesh – the only sensations I wanted him to feel on his prick were those I gave with my mouth, and, when his hips began slowly to move, I pressed my hands down, trapping him.

Now he could have me. His hands were in my hair. I twisted my body so that I could undo my jeans with one hand and, in the darkness, he understood, and pulled them sharply down. I wriggled one leg free, and positioned myself over his face. His tongue grazed my panties, but they might as well not have been there, I was so wet, and the cloth was so sheer. His fingers yanked the gusset aside regardless, and I felt his mouth against me, sucking my lips in, while his tongue flickered against the captive pink pussy. It felt glorious and I began to buck, feeling my clitoris jarring against his chin. For a moment, I even forgot what else I was doing, and rose up on my knees, my eyes closed, my hands on his stomach, conscious of nothing but the sensations sweeping through me. Have I ever come this fast, this way?

My hands found his prick again, began jerking him furiously, and as the first of my own shockwaves rippled through me, I leaned forward, impaling my face on his stiffness. There was no room for finesse, no thought for technique – he fucked my face as hard as I rode his, and, as my orgasm finally began to subside, I felt his beginning. His face was still buried deep within the sodden folds of my cunt; I heard his muffled moan just a split second before his cock jerked hard in the depths of my mouth, and his come spurted tart and fiery into my throat … and kept on spurting, wave upon wave of hot, heavy sauce.

I didn't even try to swallow; I parted my lips a little instead, and let my mind's eye picture the thick, creamy juice merging with my saliva, and spilling out of my mouth, trickling down his shaft for me to suck back in, lapping it up then sucking him dry, feeling him soften in my mouth, while spit and spunk dripped down my chin. In my dreams – fantasies – my lover films me as I do that to him, and then we watch it back on a big-screen TV. I've only ever seen it done like that in porn movies, and usually only old-time ones – modern film-makers are so obsessed with the come-shot into the mouth that they've forgotten that the best ones are the ones that come out of it. Forget hitting rewind on the remote control, though. I watch it frame by frame.

I just wished it wasn't so dark that Ryan missed seeing it as well – then realised that it wasn't. As I opened my eyes, it was to find the morning light streaming into the

146

van, and Ryan gazing at me with an expression that hovered somewhere between total ecstasy and absolute astonishment. He gasped a breathless 'wow', and that was enough. I wondered if he had a video camera.

Outside, all was birdsong, and the first stirrings of the morning traffic on the freeway outside the park. My watch said 5.40 a.m. I pulled my jeans back on and waited while Ryan did the same.

'Shall we take a look around outside?'

He nodded, and I opened the back door of the van.

'Anything?' He joined me at the opening.

I shrugged. 'Maybe a bit more garbage than I remember seeing last night, but that's about it.'

The dew-soaked grass looked lush and springy; there were no trampled pathways beyond the ones that we created ourselves, as we stepped out of the van and walked around the clearing. The little flags that marked out the dimensions of the old Ghost Train hung forlornly awaiting the morning's first breeze. Whatever we'd heard – or thought we'd heard – the previous night, it hadn't left a mark on the landscape. In fact, as he drove me home and we laughed about it, it was very easy to put the whole thing down to a healthy dose of imagination, mixed in with wishful thinking and a dash of sexual chemistry. That's what Ryan reckoned, anyway, and it made perfect sense to agree with him.

Except my ninety-something-year-old grandmother

pulled that comfort away when I went to visit her the following afternoon, and she bent down to pick up a piece of street litter that was tracked in, stuck to one of my sneakers. 'Adams Black Jack chewing gum,' she read off the pale-blue wrapper that she held in one hand. 'Oh my, I haven't seen that since I was a little girl. My brother used to chew it before he was killed in the World War.'

The First World War. The one that ended in 1918.

'They must have started making it again, Gran.' I smiled. 'You know what people are like for nostalgia. Here, let me take it. I'll drop it in the kitchen garbage on my way to the bathroom.'

Instead, I slipped it into my purse, to show to Ryan the next time I saw him. So, sexual chemistry chews vintage gum, does it?

*Fancy a F**k?*
Lisette Ashton

'Fancy a fuck?'

As chat-up lines went, I thought it had to be the cheesiest one I'd ever heard. It was coarse, vulgar and obscenely inappropriate – even for a prison. Admittedly Sid delivered the words with panache, and his boyish good looks lent him a charming appeal that was almost angelic, but the statement was so uncouth it demanded a sharp rebuttal, if not a slap across the face.

Which is why I couldn't really believe it when I heard myself say, 'OK.'

I was visiting the local women's prison at the time, a member of the Volunteer Visitors Group, and donating my time and a sympathetic ear to those unfortunates who were benefiting society by staying behind bars. My session had just finished for the day and I had spent a pleasant hour discussing the vagaries of Mozart's operas with a charming young lady serving five years for GBH.

Sid made his pass at me as I passed the window of the visiting office.

I acquiesced in the toilets labelled VISITORS: GENTS.

He didn't bother trying to undress me. Bolting his mouth against mine, pushing me back against the wall of a lavatory cubicle, he fumbled with his pants and released a hard, throbbing erection. The sight of his pulsing pink flesh, the dome swollen and the end dewy and slick with arousal, made me giddy with need. When he tugged up the hem of my skirt, I pushed my pelvis against him. He only had to pull the crotch of my panties aside and then he was sliding easily into my pussy. Neither of us seemed to understand where the rush of wetness had come from. I certainly hadn't felt particularly aroused while discussing *Die Zauberflöte*. But my inner muscles yielded to Sid as though they were freshly greased.

His kisses were blended with light nibbles that sired twinges of pain. Anxious to show him that I could be just as demanding, I chewed on his lower lip while riding myself along his shaft. He pounded hard into my sex and I responded with equal, urgent vigour. My labia had never felt so responsive. Every nuance of his length trembled through my clitoris. Rubbing myself along the veins and pulses of his cock, I was amazed by the wealth of pleasure that reverberated through my hole. The passion and exertion left me weak and greedy for climax.

Sid made a half-hearted attempt to fondle my breasts but, because we were standing in a lavatory cubicle, that wasn't wholly practical. It was more useful for him to grab my buttocks, keep the nuisance of my skirt aside with his wrists and help me to ride my pelvis to and fro along his hardness. One hand strayed to where our bodies met, the tip of his finger teased my pussy lips as he continued to plough in and out, and then I was shocked to find him touching my anus. The ring of muscle recoiled as though it had been brushed by an electric charge. A convulsion of raw desire bristled through my loins.

I squeezed my pussy muscles around him.

'How'd you like to feel my finger up your arse?' he grunted.

'I'd rather feel your cock up there,' I returned.

And he obliged.

Our climaxes occurred with his shaft buried deep into my anus.

It was a sublime experience.

There was no threat or warning that either of us was nearing our peak. Sid simply pushed himself deep through the muscle of my sphincter – I savoured the heady rush of experiencing that particular first – and then we were both struggling to contain the cries of our orgasms. His burning seed splashed hot and slick into my bowel. The muscles of his length went into repeated spasms. And the convulsions of my sphincter finally spat his used shaft out of my rear.

Thinking back to that first time, I can see now that the sex on that occasion was pretty much a reflection of how our relationship went. The whole affair was spontaneous, it was always unconventional, and we were constantly competing to outdo each other.

'Would it turn you on watching me fuck another woman?' he asked a month later.

We had exchanged names and addresses and fallen into the routine of seeing each other every night. I was trying hard not to appear too eager for him. His cocksure confidence didn't need fuelling by displays of my desire for more. But he filled me with a need that no other man had ever awoken. Meeting in strange bars, spending time at either my home or his flat, allowed me to discover a level of fulfilment I had never imagined was attainable. The arrogant bastard was everything I had ever wanted in a man.

At the time, I remember thinking that he had possessed me.

'Well?' Sid asked, prompting me from my reverie. 'Give me an answer. Would it turn you on watching me fuck another woman?'

I shrugged and thought about the proposition. It was easy to picture his length working its way in and out of another woman and, with only a little use of my imagination, I could almost hear her cries of delight as he brought her to orgasm. The idea sent a wicked thrill trembling through my pussy so I responded honestly.

'Yeah. I guess it would turn me on. Why?'

'I was wanting to bone Julie,' he explained.

Julie shared a flat with me, and had done since we attended college together. While I'd studied English, Julie had taken a degree in mediaeval literature. We were best friends and as close as sisters but the idea of my sharing a boyfriend with her was something I had never contemplated.

'Set her up for me,' Sid insisted. He grinned and added, 'You can watch us do the nasty. If you're willing, I might even let you join in.'

Again it was his confrontational tone of voice – the unspoken suggestion that I would either refuse or turn prudish – that dictated my response. I couldn't back down from the challenge of his suggestion. I shrugged and, in a voice that was almost belligerent, said, 'OK.'

And, as it turned out, it wasn't like Julie needed much in the way of persuading.

She had been anxious to meet my new boyfriend and leapt at the invitation to share a drink and a dinner date with us at his apartment. Sid and I had discussed various strategies while we fucked, each scenario bringing me to a deeper and more satisfying level of euphoria. He made a couple of suggestions about handcuffs and rope, while I thought we would stand a better chance with the simple use of lots of red wine and flattering conversation about all those interesting studies she could discuss relating to *Beowulf* and Chaucer.

As it turned out, we didn't need anything so exotic or manipulative.

I was in the kitchen, listening to Sid and Julie laugh together while I put the finishing touches to a light supper. The wine had flowed freely, although a lot of that was down to Julie's natural appetite for claret. Sid was at his charming best, making her guffaw with a heartiness that bordered on being unladylike. And, with the radio tuned to a jazz station, the combination of easy music and the smell of warm food created an ambience that was almost pedestrian in its homeliness.

Then I heard Sid ask his trademark question. 'Fancy a fuck?'

I held my breath, listening for Julie's answer. Even though I wasn't in the room I could picture the indifferent shrug of her shoulders before she nodded and responded.

'OK.'

I came back to the room and found Sid thrusting into her as she bent over the dining table. He had pushed Julie's skirt back to expose her buttocks. He was sliding into the sopping hole of her sex. I realised that I was staring at Julie's bare backside, and watching my boyfriend's erection glide in and out of her pussy. Julie and I exchanged a knowing grin before I returned to the kitchen and turned the oven down. The light supper we had scheduled was put on hold and I returned just as Julie screamed with delight. Sid was buried deep inside her, holding himself rigid as they both spat their respective expletives.

'You could have waited for me,' I complained gently.

Julie glanced over her shoulder. Her grin was a form of coquettish apology that made her look like a chastened girl. The act would have been convincing if she hadn't chosen that moment to squeeze the muscles of her sex and spit Sid's spent shaft from her hole. A dribble of oyster-white semen trailed from the pink split of her pussy. I watched and my stomach folded with an arousal so intense it made me nauseous.

Sid turned to me and pointed at his limp shaft. 'Blow me hard,' he demanded. 'I want to fuck Julie again. I can do that if you blow me.'

I heard the words but the harsh instruction was almost too much. Sid lit himself a cigar and blew a thick plume of smoke in the air before repeating his instruction. 'Blow me,' he insisted. 'Don't make me tell you a third time.'

I got down on my knees and did as he asked.

The knowledge that I was licking Julie's pussy juice from his length sent violent shivers trembling through my sex. All the kinky games and lurid fantasies that Sid and

I had shared paled into insignificance against the reality of lapping Julie's effluvia from his gradually stiffening cock. The acrid taste of feminine musk and the salt of his spend blended to make an intoxicating cocktail.

From the corner of my eye I could see that Julie remained on the dining table. She had changed position and was sitting cross-legged so she could watch everything with avaricious intent.

She and Sid shared his cigar.

Julie was seemingly untroubled that she was presented naked and used in front of me. She unfastened her blouse to reveal nipples that were hard with obvious excitement. Knowing that she was equally anxious for me to get Sid's erection back to full strength drove my arousal to a deeper plateau. I took his entire length into my mouth and sucked as ferociously as I could manage. The muscle of his erection began to throb.

'No!'

Sid snatched a fistful of my hair and pulled my head away. I glanced meekly up at him, wondering if I had hurt him or crossed some unspecified line. He held the cigar between his teeth, his grin looking almost demonic as he glared down at me.

'Nearly too much,' he grunted.

A glance at his erection told me he was already back to his full, adorable length but he didn't allow me to savour the sight.

'And, since I can tell you're gagging to taste my spunk,' he continued, 'why don't I let you sate your appetite before I fuck Julie again?'

For an instant I stared at him without comprehension.

It was only when I followed the line of his gaze, and saw he was looking at the stream of come that dribbled from Julie's sex, that I realised what he expected. I can't honestly say I would have refused – I hadn't refused one of his instructions up to that point and I didn't think I would have done then – but I do know I hesitated.

Sid didn't allow me any more vacillation. He still held my hair and rudely pushed my face against her sex. I was almost smothered by the sodden labia that engulfed my lips and nose, drowning in a musk of my lover's spunk and my flatmate's arousal. I began to splutter at first, gasping for air and struggling to breathe, and then I was licking the soft folds of her pussy lips and gently teasing Julie's clitoris. She came while I had my tongue inside her hole and I felt the trembling muscles shiver through my mouth.

Sid made that night memorable, taking Julie twice more and satisfying me with his fingers and mouth. Julie returned the pleasure I had given and I was disturbed, and enthralled, to enjoy an orgasm from her tongue slipping inside my hole and over my clitoris.

I screamed with the pleasure and passed out.

When consciousness returned to me, Sid and Julie

were talking while they shared a fresh cigar. They lay in a loose embrace.

She stroked one hand against his sac.

He tugged absently on one of her nipples.

'Does she know you're a fallen angel?'

Sid shrugged. 'If she knows, she doesn't care.'

Convulsions of pleasure still shivered through my body and I happily lay beneath their conversation, enjoying their nearness. We were all naked, there were no limitations on what we might do together, and the endless possibilities made my inner muscles shiver at the prospect of further pleasure. Their talk of fallen angels only seemed like another facet of the surreal lifestyle I had now discovered.

'You're an incubus, aren't you?'

He grinned, clearly surprised and pleased by her recognition. 'That's a very astute observation. Most people think we incubi only appear in wet dreams. How did you figure it out?'

'I've studied some mediaeval literature. You're mentioned in *Malleus Maleficarum*,' Julie explained. 'At first I thought you might be a lust demon, someone like Asmodeus maybe, but, despite the fact that you're a bastard, you seem like a considerate lover. That's the sign of a true fallen angel.'

She snorted back a giggle, coughed lightly on the cigar and stroked the flaccid length between his legs. With a knowing smile, she asked, 'Is it true that you can affect your own size?'

His laughter was polite and almost embarrassed. It was a strange sound to come from Sid's mouth.

'You're an insatiable little bitch, aren't you?' he grunted, making no attempt to move her hand, his smile growing broader as she stroked her fingers back and forth along the length of his shaft.

Julie waved his comment aside. 'Do you plan to get her pregnant? Isn't that what you incubi do?'

'Myth,' he said simply. 'Like all the angels except Gabriel, I'm firing blanks. Also, unless she has ovaries in her bowel, there's been little chance of my impregnating her since we first met.'

Julie nodded and took the cigar from between his fingers.

'Have you hypnotised her?' she asked.

She was either unaware that I had regained consciousness or quite content to speak about me as though I was unable to hear. She also seemed happy for Sid to suck on her nipple and finger both her holes while she smoked his cigar.

'You've got her doing depraved things she wouldn't ordinarily do,' Julie continued. A rasp of arousal underscored her words. 'Is my best friend under the thrall of some spell that you're weaving?'

He laughed and took the cigar from her. 'I've hypnotised

159

both of you,' he explained coolly. 'My hold over her is obviously stronger. But for tonight, and every other night that I deem it to be so, you're under my spell too.'

Julie seemed untroubled by the revelation.

As was I.

If I hadn't thought it would spoil the mood of the conversation I would have fingered myself as I watched them.

'Why?' she asked simply. 'Why are you doing this to her?'

I strained to hear, anxious to discover his motives before I carried on surrendering to him.

'Why?' he repeated. 'You're the student of mediaeval literature. I thought you would have known. I'm an incubus. I'm a fallen angel. I've committed the unforgivable sin of loving mortal women so I'm now condemned to roam the earth. It's now my vocation to seduce innocents like her and introduce them to corruption and acts of minor larceny.'

'Haven't you corrupted her enough?' Julie asked.

He drew on the cigar and shook his head while savouring the smoke. 'Of course I haven't corrupted her enough,' he chided gently. 'But I'm getting there.'

Later, Sid explained his plans while we simply nodded blithe acceptance. He told us about his life as a fallen angel and the frustration of being punished for the mere crime of loving mortal women. It was a pithy speech that made his lust and depravity seem noble and almost dignified. Then we smoked another of his cigars and Sid butt-fucked us alternately, while we writhed together beneath him.

Sid and I shared our relationship with Julie a couple more times before she eventually said the ménage was creepy. I never knew if it was an exercise in willpower or if Sid had grown bored with her, but she eventually stopped accepting our invitations for light suppers. By that time I guess Sid and I were into bigger thrills than threesomes.

I found it easy to forget about Sid's supernatural revelations and, when Julie denounced our relationship as unholy and ungodly, it merely looked like a laughable attempt at reclaiming a virtue she had never possessed. I remember thinking that she had plucked the phrase from one of the dry tomes of medieval literature that she was always pretending to study.

'Where do you want to go today?' he asked one evening.

The summer had come with a rush of sweltering days and long, leisurely twilights. The clement weather appealed to the outdoorsman in Sid's nature and he had coaxed me into fucking him in unusual and daring locations. I hadn't realised they were daring at first – a shopping precinct and a car park didn't seem that bold – but when Sid pointed out that we were being watched by CCTV cameras I realised the risk we were courting. Fresh excitement boiled through my loins when I understood the consequences we faced if our indiscretions ever came to light. And none of those considerations stopped me from letting him fuck me rigid beneath the watchful eye of the CCTV cameras.

'You don't say no to much, do you?' he remarked one evening.

I could have argued, and pointed out that so far in our relationship I hadn't said no to anything. But I was in a mood to play it cool.

'Should I be saying no to something?'

'I bet you'll say no to my suggestion for tonight.'

He was taunting me – daring me to refuse and knowing I wouldn't. I remained nonchalant and said, 'You're right. I probably will say no. What did you have in mind?'

'I want to fuck you in a jewellery shop.'

'Is that all?'

'We'll have to break in …'

'So?'

'… and there's a risk we could get caught.'

'To which part of this did you expect me to say no?'

We didn't talk on the journey down to the jewellers. I was driving and Sid had one of my breasts in his mouth while his fingers squirmed inside my pussy. My arousal was furious, making his hand squelch wetly as he teased me to climax. But, although it was awkward to handle the car, we got there safely. He kissed me outside the jewellery shop, his tongue plundering my mouth and making me hot enough to moan for him to take me. When he asked if I was ready, all I could do was sigh with agreement.

Sid used a hammer to smash through the window. Then he carried me inside. Alarm bells clattered and whooped at a volume that hurt.

But I barely noticed those distractions.

Sid was laying me across a glass-topped display counter and pushing his cock between my legs. I don't know how long he rode me.

The moment seemed both instantaneous and infinite.

His shaft was buried deep inside me and he pounded away at my sex until I was aching from the pain of repeated orgasms. Doubled over in agony I waited for him to squirt deep into my pussy before allowing him to drag me out of the shop. Police sirens were becoming audible over the wail of the jeweller's alarm and I knew Sid had timed our encounter to perfection. I also knew, when he asked if we should try that again, I wasn't going to refuse.

Don't think me stupid. I knew he was stealing from the shop, but I couldn't see any reason to complain. I was quite happy for him to break the windows, and I was more than delighted to have him pump me full of his demonic seed each time we found a new shop to use. If

I'd bothered to rationalise any of it in my mind I would have called it a victimless crime. Insurance companies would pay the shops for their broken windows and lost wares, and we were even giving the police something to do of an evening other than patrol the local drunk spots.

Trouble only started when Sid asked me if I wanted to use the hammer.

The idea excited me. I had watched him smash the windows and I had been thrilled by the way the implement worked as a crude switch to activate the alarms. The prospect of being responsible for that delicious clatter of noise was too tempting and I jumped at the offer. I smashed the window, basked in the glorious noise and had the strongest orgasm I could recall experiencing. The pleasure was so intense I was on the brink of losing consciousness when my climax came. It was only when Sid shook me back to reality that I realised I had almost spoiled our fun permanently by blacking out in a haze of post-coital pleasure.

'We have to go,' he bawled.

He was struggling to make himself heard over the cry of the alarm and let me know we had overstayed our welcome. Sid held my hand and tried pulling me from the counter where I lay.

'We have to leave now.'

'You're not going anywhere,' a security officer announced.

Wearing a dark uniform, holding a set of handcuffs and wincing from the noise of the shrieking alarms, the security officer stepped closer. He placed a meaty hand on my shoulder and I understood that the run of fun I'd enjoyed with Sid was now over.

Sid shook his head. He glanced at the omnipotent eye of the CCTV cameras and then me. I understood I would be centre stage on the security monitors recording the situation.

Sid's gaze met mine and he said, 'I hope you do fancy a fuck, darling, because we're truly fucked now.'

'What's your problem?' I demanded.

The alarms were adding to my panic. I tried to struggle and free myself from the man holding my shoulder but his grip was firm and unyielding. He slapped a handcuff on my wrist and when he attached the other cuff to his own hand I realised I was caught.

'I thought you approved of the occasional small crime?' I said to Sid. 'You're a demon. A devil. A fallen angel. I thought you encouraged minor acts of larceny and corruption?'

He rolled his eyes, clearly exasperated. 'Minor acts of corruption meet with my approval,' he growled. 'But we're going to be charged here with conspiracy, premeditated, and several other variations of theft and robbery.' He shook his head sadly and said, 'You've fucked us, darling.'

Except Sid wasn't fucked.

I told him to go – and he went.

I never revealed his name or identity to the police, and I claimed all responsibility for the spate of robberies. Of course they knew I hadn't acted alone. They'd seen enough CCTV footage of Sid and me fucking during the robberies to be certain of that much, and the security guard was happy to tell his superiors everything he could remember about our parting conversation.

But, without any clue to who Sid was, there was nothing they could do.

Nothing, that is, except make an example of me and put me in prison for a long time.

* * *

Sid has just finished visiting.

I can see him now, making his way out with the other visitors. He's still enjoying the freedom that I gave him. It was good to talk with him today and the only thing that makes me sad is that I heard what he said to one of the female visitors. He just asked her if she fancied a fuck. And, when I saw the smile reflected in her eyes, I knew how she was going to reply.

The Hunt
Penelope Hildern

'It's the fear that's so exhilarating.'

Niall looked up. 'Fear?'

John nodded at William, who had spoken. Both men shared a smile, like members of a secret society.

When they didn't elaborate, Niall turned back to the fire, feeling left out. He hadn't seen either of his old friends since school. That was ten years ago and he'd been surprised when John had emailed him out of the blue, inviting him to stay at Lakestone for the weekend.

John's father had recently died and left him the country estate. As a boy John had been denied by his eccentric parents the pleasures and privileges that should have come with such wealth. He'd never been taken abroad with them on their exotic travels, never been given flashy cars or other fripperies. The three boys had often spun wild fantasies about what they would do if they were

167

kings of the castle. Now it looked like John was making a start on his own empire.

They sat in the lavish drawing room, drinking booze that was older than their combined ages. Dinner had been a bacchanalian feast with more dishes than Niall could count and more pudding than he could eat. He was pleasantly buzzed and too full to move. He'd already forgotten about Tina and her need for 'more space' and 'room to think'.

At school the boys had been like brothers and he felt bad about losing touch. But John had tracked him down at just the right time. Tina could have all the space she wanted while Niall reminisced with his old friends and relived past glories. There was certainly no way he was going to turn down an invitation to participate in what John had called 'that most decadent of gentlemanly pursuits – the hunt'. The fact that he'd never ridden a horse or fired a gun or killed anything larger than a spider was no hindrance. John assured him that he would catch on in no time.

William had apparently been out to Lakestone before on such hunts but, when pressed by Niall about what it was like, would only offer him a cryptic smile. 'Trust me,' he'd said, 'you'll love it.'

It seemed a little strange to Niall that it was just the three of them for a hunt, but in truth he was glad. A larger group would have been intimidating and only make him feel like an outsider.

'The fear and the inevitability,' John said suddenly, picking up the thread again.

This time Niall was determined not to be excluded. 'Fear of what?'

Both men turned to him with identical expressions. Their eyes gleamed with excitement, as though it was all they could do to keep from letting slip some delicious secret.

'The fear of being caught, of course,' John said. 'Knowing it's going to happen and being powerless to do anything about it.'

Niall smiled, understanding at last. 'Ah, you mean for the fox! But surely it doesn't know it will be caught. The fear is merely an instinctive flight response to being chased.'

The teasing smile came again and Niall wondered if he'd said something foolish. Or were his friends plotting some bit of mischief?

His concerns must have been written on his face because John laughed and clapped him on the shoulder. 'Don't worry,' he said, 'there's no practical joke at your expense. You'll understand tomorrow.'

Niall sighed with relief and tried not to look as though he'd been dreading exactly that.

'Well, early to bed, lads,' William said, punctuating his words with an extravagant yawn. 'We'll need all our strength tomorrow.'

'Without question,' John added. 'Niall, why don't you take the Chinese room? Up the stairs, third door on the right.'

Niall found it after quite a bit of searching and his eyes widened when he saw the room. It looked like a film set from some period drama. Green and red silk hangings adorned the walls, along with red paper lanterns. Gold dragon statuettes stood proudly on the fireplace mantel and the room was dominated by an enormous black lacquered bed with intricately carved slats.

But none of that was what made him gape. Rather incongruously, an enormous cage hung from a heavy iron hook in the window bay. It looked like a giant version of a dainty Victorian birdcage and it seemed out of place in the otherwise soft and silky room. Presumably it had once housed some exotic parrot or perhaps even a falcon. But how cruel to hang the creature before the window, with such a spectacular view of the rolling hills and trees of the estate.

He recalled the stories about Lakestone he'd heard as a child, the murmurs about mysterious goings-on in the woods and the secretive nature of John's parents whenever the boys had gone there to play. Villagers claimed that the woods were enchanted, that the faerie folk came out to play tricks on unwary travellers who ventured within. And on one occasion Niall was convinced he'd seen fantastic creatures frolicking in a clearing.

'Just your imagination,' he'd been told then. And his own common sense had eventually prevailed. Of course. What else could it have been?

Over time the memory had faded and now he could barely remember what he thought he'd seen that day. Although he'd never completely shaken the sense that there was something unusual about the woods.

It was some time before Niall was able to sleep. When he did he dreamed of foxes and hounds and the sound of a huntsman's horn.

* * *

'Where are the horses?'

'No horses,' John said, springing open the latches of a large leather case. 'No hounds either.'

'Then how –'

'So many questions! Honestly, my dear boy, you'll spoil the surprise.'

'Surprise?'

John pressed an oddly shaped pistol into Niall's hand. 'Surprise,' he said firmly. 'Trust me.' He winked and turned to William. 'Now I'm red, as always. William, you're green. And, Niall, that makes you blue.'

Niall looked at the weapon in confusion before realisation dawned. It was a paintball gun. Surprise? Were they to hunt one another? He felt a wave of disappointment.

He'd spent the days leading up to this weekend in delirious anticipation, like a child waiting for Christmas morning, only to find that it wasn't to be a proper hunt after all.

William was taking practice aim at the trees with his gun and when he caught Niall watching he gave him a lascivious wink. Perhaps William was merely humouring John's apparent madness and once the 'hunt' began he would slip off to the local pub.

'Right,' John said, as if all was clear now. He blew three short bursts on a whistle around his neck. 'To the hunt, gentlemen!'

With that, he took off running towards the woods and, with a mock salute, William went in the opposite direction, across the open grounds.

Niall stood where he was, baffled. Then he shook his head in resignation and decided to head for the little stream he could see at the base of the hill.

He took his time walking, still suspecting that it was all some schoolboy prank. But it was a lovely day and, if nothing else, he could enjoy the simple pleasure of being out in the countryside, away from the noise and smoke of London and the knowledge that he and Tina were finished. The sunny weather went some way towards soothing his disappointment. Paintball indeed.

When he reached the stream he thought he caught the sound of running feet and he froze, listening. The sound came again, from a little copse of trees off to his left. Quietly he made his way towards it, listening intently. In spite of everything, his heart pounded with excitement, the primal thrill of the hunt.

The silence was too conspicuous to be natural. Something was hiding in the bushes. He crept closer and was rewarded with the rustling of leaves as whatever it was tried to move into deeper cover. Niall inched closer, following. There was another rustle and then suddenly an animal burst from the undergrowth and ran towards the stream. Niall's heart caught in his throat. No, not an animal. A *girl*.

She was naked but for the extravagant feathers that adorned her arms and the long bronze plume of a tail that flowed out behind her. Around her neck was a ring of brilliant white and her eyes were hidden by a scarlet mask, as though she'd escaped from some lavish costume ball. And all at once Niall understood the game. He stared after the lovely pheasant in wonderment for only a minute before giving chase.

She didn't glance back at him, but ran in a wild zig-zag pattern. He half expected the magnificent bird to take flight, so convincing was her attire. He got off a shot and a glut of blue paint struck a nearby tree as his pheasant easily outpaced him and vanished into the woods. He ran after her but she proved too quick and nimble and before long she was out of sight.

But now that he knew the secret behind the hunt he was on his guard. He sneaked through the trees, listening carefully for any sound, watching for any tiny flash of colour.

He soon came to a small glade and he blinked in surprise to see a trestle table positioned there. On it were scattered what looked like gemstones. It took him a moment to realise that they were chocolates wrapped in brightly coloured foil. Ah, the perfect bait for such prey! And now that he looked closer he could see some sort of wire encircling the table at its base, concealed by drifts of leaves and flowers. Niall managed to contain his laugh of delight as he secreted himself behind a tree to wait.

It wasn't long before he was rewarded. The snap of a dry twig alerted him to the presence of some new quarry and he froze where he was. Sure enough, there soon came the sound of dainty footsteps as something approached the glade.

A sleek, slender figure emerged from the camouflage of the trees and Niall held his breath as the girl came into view. This one was a deer. And she was a vision. Her long limbs and body had been painted a warm tawny brown that emphasised her lean, athletic physique. Her hands and feet were painted black to resemble delicate hooves and when she turned away to glance behind her Niall saw the flick of a little white tail above her heart-shaped bottom.

174

She picked her way towards the table with all the grace of the creature she was emulating, her deep-black eyes scanning the glade for any sign of threat, her costume ears pricked as though she might actually be listening with them. Her body seemed to be vibrating with energy, with a wary anticipation that she might be caught at any moment. Niall remembered what his friends had said the night before about how the fear was so exhilarating.

He slowly raised his gun, determined not to let this one get away. But, even as he fired, she triggered the wire beneath the table and a net sprang up from behind her. It closed over her like a mouth and she gave a little cry as she found herself caught. She flailed helplessly with her arms and legs but she only succeeded in tangling herself further in the knotted mesh.

Her left hip and side were coated with bright-blue paint and Niall grew even more excited at the thought that she was now marked as his. He approached her with the same caution he would have used with a real animal he'd just captured. He held out his hands in a calming gesture and her eyes went wide as she saw him. A moment later her surprise dissolved into a shy smile and she lowered her head. She ceased her struggles and sank to her knees as he drew near.

A wave of arousal swept over him at this gesture of submission. He stood over her and began working to free her from the net. She held out each limb obediently so he could untangle it from the mesh and once he had done so she made no move to escape. Instead, she stayed on her knees and merely watched him, a shy smile dancing in her liquid black eyes.

Her long dark hair was pulled back away from her face and secured by a headband onto which had been stitched a pair of large velvety ears. Her dainty nose had been painted black, emphasising her high cheekbones and soft, full lips.

'Well, my little doe,' Niall said at last, 'what am I to do with you?'

The deer girl peered up at him, biting her lip with an expression of eager anticipation. It was clearly up to him.

He moved away a few paces and beckoned her forwards. She came to him on all fours like an obedient pet and knelt again at his feet. His cock stirred. He moved away again, this time towards the table. Her face brightened as he scooped up a handful of the chocolates and unwrapped one. Then he held it out to her.

Again she crept towards him on her hands and knees, stretching out her long neck for the treat. She dipped her head and ate from his hand, her soft lips brushing his palm.

'Good girl,' Niall said, reaching down to stroke her.

She sighed contentedly and lowered her head even more so he could caress the back of her neck. Then she raised one elegant arm and pawed softly at the ground before beseeching him with a hungry look. He indulged her with another chocolate and this time she licked his palm, nibbling gently at the pads of his fingers. His cock felt like it would burst from his trousers and this time when he tempted her to follow him he removed his jacket and spread it down on the ground.

At this the girl's expression grew even more submissive. She gazed up at him from beneath her long dark lashes for a moment before she crept to the makeshift bed and lay back on it. Her painted body was a work of art, enhanced rather than marred by the splash of cobalt blue across her left hip.

'You're beautiful,' Niall whispered.

The deer girl offered him another shy smile before unfolding her long legs to reveal the moist pink lips of her sex. She didn't need to say a word. Her eyes told him everything he needed to know.

He undressed quickly, his cock beginning to ache with need as the girl writhed on the ground before him, angling her legs apart and drawing her hands down across her breasts. Her nipples hardened into stiff little peaks.

Niall knelt between her legs and bent down over her, trying to decide where to touch her first. At last his hands cupped her face and he pressed his lips to hers. Her tongue immediately sought his and he murmured with pleasure at the taste of chocolate. He drew his hands down along her body, feeling the swell of her breasts and circling his thumbs lazily over her nipples. She gasped at the stimulation, reaching out to either side to clutch at the edges of his jacket beneath her. She threw back her head with a gasp as he kneaded her breasts, rolling the sensitive nipples between his fingers.

Her breathing grew fast and shallow and she forced her legs even further apart, raising her head to offer him another pleading look. He knew what she wanted, what they both wanted, but he was determined to make the experience last as long as possible. He was teasing himself as much as her.

As she writhed beneath him he continued to explore her with his hands, drawing his fingers down over her lithe, flexible body, admiring the tautness of her muscles, the flatness of her belly, the firmness of her skin. When he finally reached her thighs she was panting hungrily and he was sure he could actually hear her heart throbbing like that of a captured animal. Fear and the inevitability of being caught. Being powerless to do anything about it. He'd never even dared to imagine that such girls might exist!

He drew his fingers along the dewy folds of her sex and she cried out softly, tossing her head from side to side. Then he stopped for a moment to admire the sight of her again. She was completely shaved. The pinkness of her sex stood out in sharp contrast to her painted thighs. Her nether lips were swollen and glistening with arousal and he thought it was quite the most beautiful thing he'd ever seen.

Seeing his expression, the girl bent her knees and drew her legs up to her chest in a wide V, holding herself shockingly open for him. Niall was both astonished and excited by her flexibility. Her feet were nearly behind her head. He stared down at her splayed form, at the invitation of her exposed sex so fully on display. She grinned playfully, offering herself, begging him to take her.

If he forced himself to wait any longer he would burst. Niall finally positioned himself and, inch by slow inch, pushed himself deep inside her warm wet opening. Immediately she clenched herself around him, squeezing him with inner muscles he'd never known could be so powerful. She gave a delighted little laugh at his look of surprise.

Taking hold of her ankles, he braced himself against her as he began to thrust in and out. She pushed back with surprising strength and he got the message: she wanted it rougher. He obliged, pulling back and then driving himself in with one ferocious thrust after another. She cried out each time, a sound of primal passion that he imagined could be heard all the way back at the house.

It was almost too good, too perfect. Surely none of this was real. Surely he was still asleep in that decadent Chinese room, in that lacquered cage of a bed, dreaming this entire experience.

But there was the silky feel of her, the tightness of her sex, the incredible elasticity of her limbs, not to mention those bottomless black eyes urging him on. No, it was no dream. She was real, every exquisite inch of her.

From the corner of his eye he saw the glint of sunlight on the coloured jewels of chocolate on the table and he suddenly wanted to have her from behind. He withdrew slowly and her eyes went wide with surprise. But she was reassured when he pulled her to her feet and led her to the table. He pushed her forwards and she melted across the surface, taking hold of the far edge and peering back over her shoulder at Niall.

He smiled as he lifted her little white tail and spread her burnished cheeks apart. Some of the makeup had rubbed off and he imagined that he was stripping her of the beast within, taming her. She held still for him as he positioned himself and entered her again. With an ecstatic gasp she tossed her head, arching her back. Her feet left the ground and she wrapped her legs around him from behind, locking her ankles together in the small of his back and tensing her powerful thigh muscles against him.

He moaned with pleasure as he took her again, relishing the sight of her long, sleek back and her desperately clutching hands on the edge of the table as he pounded into her, eliciting breathless cries. The force of his thrusts knocked her headband askew and her hair came free in wild dark tangles. He smelled the rich creamy scent of chocolate

180

as the treats were crushed beneath her. The thought of licking her clean was all he needed to send him over the edge. He came so hard his ears rang and he thought he might actually faint from the intensity. The girl held herself still beneath him as his body throbbed and pulsed.

When it was over he stumbled back from the table. The girl remained where she was for a moment before rolling onto her back and smiling up at him. There was something impish in her smile and Niall saw that she held one of the chocolates in her hand. She had smashed it in her fist and now she smeared the melted substance over her breasts and sex like some kind of tribal warpaint.

Incredibly, his cock was already stirring again at the sight. He kissed each chocolatey nipple before parting her thighs and lowering his mouth to the tiny sensitive place that craved his attention most of all. Each flick of his tongue across her clitoris made her twitch and gasp and it wasn't long before her body convulsed with pleasure and she loosed a wild cry into the trees as she came.

After a few moments she rolled onto her side, curled into a foetal position and smiled at him, her eyes dazed and blissful. He had the sense that, like him, she was only temporarily sated, that she would want more very soon. He also had the sense that she knew exactly what he was thinking.

'You caught me,' she said at last in a soft voice. 'That means I belong to you for the night.'

Niall hadn't been expecting her to speak and his face must have borne the same expression of surprise as if an actual deer had just spoken.

She laughed, a high musical sound. Then she sat up and swung her legs off the table. 'I was hoping it would be you,' she continued. 'We saw you arrive yesterday and I told the others that I hoped you would be the one to catch me.'

'Others?'

'Mmm, yes. Others. You saw Ava, I think. The pheasant? There's a fox too. And a couple of other animals you wouldn't normally find in this country.'

Niall's cock strained at the picture his mind was creating. He imagined a row of cages, each containing some fantastic female specimen disguised as a different animal to be chased and caught. What had she said? That she belonged to him for the night? He suddenly remembered the cage in his bedroom. More importantly, the sturdy iron hook it hung from. And like a vision of the future he saw his little deer there, her long powerful limbs bound, her lean body suspended before him as he cleaned her, wiping her down with a sponge as she struggled feebly and sighed with pleasure at the sensation of warm water sluicing away the body paint and chocolate.

Afterwards he would carry her to the bed and acquaint himself with her human form, enjoying the warm salty taste of her skin as she lay bound and helpless before him. And if she struggled too much or disobeyed him, he might have to put her in the cage until she had learned her lesson.

The girl's eyes gleamed as she searched his face with a teasing smile, as though she could see the little fantasy he was playing out in his mind.

'Come on,' he said, taking her by the hand. 'We have a long night ahead of us.'

* * *

When Niall finally came down for breakfast the next morning his friends greeted him with knowing smiles. He hadn't closed his eyes all night but the girl had finally drifted into a blissful sleep after a particularly devastating orgasm, her fourth of the evening.

'I don't suppose we need to ask you how it went with Fawn,' John said.

Niall grinned. Fawn. So that was her name. Neither of them had even thought about such banalities as names; they'd been too busy exploring one another's body and most creative fantasies. He sighed contentedly at the memory of her crouching submissively in the cage, peering out at him with those huge dark eyes.

'I had a brilliant time,' William said. 'As always.' He winked at Niall. 'Bagged myself a brace of pheasants.'

'Well done,' Niall said with a laugh. 'My little deer was more than enough on her own.'

He sipped his coffee, savouring the taste as he savoured the memories of the night before. Right now the girl was lying naked on the bed, her wrists tied together. Her request. She'd told him she couldn't sleep any other way. Throughout the night he'd imagined her in other scenarios – curled in a basket at the foot of his bed, harnessed and fed sugar cubes from his hand, collared and chained, marked as his. He'd shared each fantasy with her, exciting and stimulating her and making her writhe with lust.

'Oh yes,' she'd purred. 'I want to experience every form.'

He'd thought it a peculiar thing to say at the time. For some reason she reminded him of the time he'd imagined those strange creatures in the woods. The creatures he'd been told weren't real. The creatures that didn't exist.

Before he'd been able to pursue that line of thinking, Fawn had distracted him again, showing off her astonishing flexibility as she spread her legs wider than he'd ever imagined possible. And he'd lost himself again in the mischievous sparkle in her eyes …

John startled him from his reverie. 'Niall?'

'Huh? What?'

'I was just thinking,' he said, a knowing smile playing on his lips. 'Perhaps next weekend you'd like to join me on my boat. We're going fishing down by Mermaid Cove.'

Niall closed his eyes and smiled. He could already imagine the magnificent creature he would haul from the water.